Praise for *A Questionable Shape*

- BARD FICTION PRIZE 2014
- THE BELIEVER BOOK AWARD FINALIST
- ONE OF THE BEST BOOKS OF 2013

Book Riot, Slate, The L Magazine, NPR's *On Point, Salon*

"Equal parts David Foster Wallace and Richard Matheson [...] *A Questionable Shape* is certainly the first Proustian zombie novel, but hopefully not the last horror novel of ideas." —*Slate*

"*A Questionable Shape* is a rewriting of the genre in rather literal sense... Sims' zombie novel perhaps contains the highest proportion of great descriptions of light per page since Proust."
—*Los Angeles Review of Books*

"Evokes the power of David Foster Wallace with a narrative that's cerebral, strangely beautiful, philosophical, and pretty, well, brilliant." —*Bustle*

"*A Questionable Shape* presents the yang to the yin of Whitehead's *Zone One*, with chess games, a dinner invitation, and even a romantic excursion. Echoes of [Thomas] Bernhard's hammering circularity and [David Foster] Wallace's bright mind that can't stop making connections are both present. The point is where the mind goes, and, in that respect, Sims has his thematic territory down cold." —*The Daily Beast*

"Unlike anything I'd ever read. Underlying the seemingly quirky subject matter of Sims' novel is a notable linguistic dynamism and impressive command of philosophical challenges. Sims' work has a life of its own." —*Full Stop*

"Yes, it's a zombie novel, but also an emotionally resonant meditation on memory and loss." —*San Francisco Chronicle*

"Sims demonstrates he isn't just smart—he's brilliant; his book's not beautiful—it's gorgeous. It's sensitive, insightful and ruminative, which aren't always things you get to say about zombie fiction, let alone most books." —*The L Magazine*

Bennett Sims

WHITE
DIALOGUES
STORIES

Two Dollar Radio
Books too loud to ignore

Two Dollar Radio
Books too loud to ignore

WHO WE ARE TWO DOLLAR RADIO is a family-run outfit dedicated to reaffirming the cultural and artistic spirit of the publishing industry. We aim to do this by presenting bold works of literary merit, each book, individually and collectively, providing a sonic progression that we believe to be too loud to ignore.

TWODOLLARRADIO.com

Proudly based in
Columbus
OHIO

 @TwoDollarRadio

 @TwoDollarRadio

/TwoDollarRadio

Love the
PLANET?
So do we.

Printed on Rolland Enviro, which contains 100% post-consumer fiber, is ECOLOGO, Processed Chlorine Free, Ancient Forest Friendly and FSC® certified and is manufactured using renewable biogas energy.

 PERMANENT 100% BIO GAS ENERGY   Ancient Forest Friendly™

Printed in Canada

SOME RECOMMENDED LOCATIONS FOR READING *WHITE DIALOGUES*:
A cabin in the woods; During a Hitchcock lecture; An oak escritoire at midnight; Or, pretty much anywhere because books are portable and the perfect technology!

AUTHOR PHOTOGRAPH→
by Carmen Maria Machado

COVER DESIGN→
by Two Dollar Radio

Stills from *Vertigo* used by permission of NBCUniversal, ©1958 Universal City Studios, Inc. for Samuel Taylor and Patricia Hitchcock O'Connell as trustees und. | Still from *Rear Window* used by permission of NBCUniversal, ©1954 Universal City Studios.

Versions of these stories appeared in the following publications: 'House-sitting' in *Tin House*; 'The Bookcase' in *Zoetrope: All-Story*; 'Ekphrases' in *A Public Space*; 'Two Guys Watching *Cujo* on Mute' in *Story*; 'City of Wolfmen' in *The Iowa Review*; 'Destroy All Monsters' in *Orion Magazine*; 'Fables' in *Conjunctions* and *Subtropics* (as 'The Balloon'), as well as in the *Pushcart Prize Anthology*; 'A Premonition' in *Gigantic*; 'Radical Closure' in *Conjunctions*; 'White Dialogues' in *Electric Literature's Recommended Reading*.

Bennett Sims

WHITE

DIALOGUES

STORIES

For Sam

CONTENTS

House-sitting

'Spiders as nature's craziness, I often think.'
—Thomas Bernhard, *Gargoyles*

WITHIN MOMENTS OF ARRIVING AT THE CABIN, you begin to suspect that the owner is a madman.

The place is in a state of disrepair. Isolated from the mountain town of N— by half an hour's drive, and separated from the road by a mile's hike down a narrowing footpath, the cabin is a perfect hermitage: a single-story log structure standing alone in a weedy grass field, which is itself in the middle of the mountainside's thick pine forests. Hidden from sight, the property has been allowed to dilapidate. The front yard's weeds have grown waist-high, and they advance on the cabin as far as its banister. When a wind blows to bend them, seed-gone grasses lap at the porch. And leaning close to the cabin are a couple of pine trees whose untrimmed branches rake at its roof. The cabin could not look any more like a ruin. Yet you have reason to know that it is not a ruin. A human being—the cabin's owner, your new employer—still lives in this place. If the property is disheveled, then it must mirror the dishevelment of his mind.

You have never met the owner. You have not even spoken with him over the phone. When you responded to his house-sitting advertisement, he wrote back within days, asking whether you would be available to begin immediately. He had, apparently, already left. A key would be waiting for you beneath a stone on the porch. Because you live in the foothills of the mountain, and because you had arranged no other employment for the summer, it had not been a problem for you to pack your bag that night and set out first thing in the morning. In this way you—without so much as an interview—accepted a house-sitting position in a cabin in the woods.

Once inside, you make a quick inspection of the cabin. It is not the quaint woodland cottage you had been expecting, but for just a summer it will be serviceable. In the kitchen you turn knobs at the sink, and water runs, ruddily, from the faucet. Flipping switches, you find that there is power. For the most part, the interior of the cabin exudes the same air of abandonment as the outside. Some tables and chairs, a desk. In the bedroom an unsheeted mattress, stained, lying on the floorboards. And the walls, closets, shelves, and drawers: all perversely empty. You search the living room for a book or magazine, but see nothing: only the coffee table with its three chairs, a fourth chair in the corner. And opening the drawers of the bedroom dresser, you satisfy yourself that not a single article of clothing has been left behind. There could just as well be no one living here.

Seemingly the only personal possession of the owner's are the dreamcatchers that he has strung in all the windows. Their feathered nets flash out at you from every pane. The bedroom window, naturally. But also in the small window above the kitchen sink, a dreamcatcher, and in the three windows arranged across the dining room's northern wall, dreamcatchers. Where there are panes of glass in the doors, dreamcatchers in the doors. Even in the bathroom, you pull back the shower curtain to reveal a dreamcatcher in the stall's brick-sized window. When you see it you have to laugh. The sheer excess: no glass in the cabin is unprotected by these webs. By these prophylaxes against nightmare.

Now here, you think, is a man absolutely terrified of nightmares.

When you finish unpacking your duffel bag you stand at the bedroom window, idly fingering the dreamcatcher there. Through the pane, you can see that the back lawn is equally weedy and lush as the front. Tall grasses stretch for a few hundred yards to a final stand of pines, as straight and dark as a squall line. The property ends where the forest begins, and each day the border between them must grow more blurred.

You try to imagine what sort of man would live this way. You have been assuming that the owner is older: rangy and gaunt, with a white beard and unkempt hair; retired, probably, and living out his last years on a pension, alone in hermitic reclusion. But in truth you have no idea how old he is, or how long he has been living in the cabin, or where—other than this cabin—he could even be staying right now. Nothing in the cabin suggests either that he is retired or that he isn't; that he practices a specific trade, or what that trade might be. Indeed, the only clue to the owner's identity is how completely he has avoided the usual traces or clues to identity. And from the absence of these things in the cabin, all you can infer is an absence of them in his life. You survey the empty bedroom and try to imagine him here. You picture an old, bony man, on the mattress on the floor, naked and cradling his knees to his chest—delirious with fear.

You look out the window again at the weedy yard. Yes, you think: he has done what it took to protect himself from these nightmares of his and neglected everything else. While in the meantime what really encroaches on the cabin is wilderness. Brambles and branches close in on the house, and eventually they will fold over it completely, subsuming it, the way that a tree's bark flows over a nail. That is what the cabin reminds you of, in the end: a nail. Five rooms and a roof hammered into the heart of the forest, where they wait, with the patience of a nail, to become ingrown.

The dreamcatcher hangs from a thin string tied around a bent nail, which the owner has hammered slantwise into the white wood of the window's lintel. Suspended in the center of the pane, the net is about the size of your fist, and it consists of a hoop of beige willow wood, encircling a mesh middle woven from some kind of synthetic nylon material. The threads—springy and white like basketball netting, and vertebrated with colored beads—overlap one another with the density of a spiderweb. Knotted in places are black crow feathers and pleached twigs that dangle in a fringe. The device, you know, is designed to catch and then neutralize nightmares. It is implicated, as an artifact, in systems of superstition that posit an exogenous source for dreams: some invisible stream or current, some river of imagery, that pours in like moonlight through the bedroom's window at night, and from there into the sleeper's ear. The dreamcatcher in the windowpane is meant to function as a filtration mechanism: letting through all the unpolluted, pleasant images, and collecting in its net any effluent of nightmare.

But this does not seem to be the system of superstition in which the owner is participating. If that were the case, a single dreamcatcher would suffice, strung up in the room in which he slept. Rather, the owner seems to have installed them according to a siege principle. In his sheer methodicalness, he could have been embattling his cabin against a mob. Not an inanimate nightmare, then, borne passively along on a stream of dream images, but an incubus: an active force, sentient and intent, determined to get *inside* the cabin. Probing the windowpanes for weaknesses at night, the blind groping of its dark hand. Every possible entrance has to be accounted for.

You support the hoop of the dreamcatcher in your palm, and the webbing goes slack and limp, draping over your hand like a bolas. When you play your fingers up and down, this tangles your hand even further. Clearly the owner is obsessed: paranoid, fixated, deluded on the matter of nightmares. But less clear, at this moment, are the particular beliefs that have structured that obsession, the private logic or mythology he has evolved.

You have never had a nightmare that you still feared after waking—never one so vivid that it made you reluctant to go back to sleep, much less one that made you pace from room to room, hammering in place a barricade of dreamcatchers. Twisting your hand, you extricate it at last from the webbing and release the hoop. It clatters back in place against the glass.

The owner has provided you neither a number nor an address at which he can be reached, not even in case of emergency. And on the fourth day in a row that you drive to his barren postal box in downtown N——, you give up any expectation of receiving further instructions from him. But it is true that all your needs are met. The owner has left half the amount of your cash stipend in a white envelope on the kitchen counter, just as his letter promised. This amount can be made to last until he returns, at which point, you suppose, you have no reason to doubt that he will pay you the rest.

By the end of the first week, you have fallen into a routine. In the mornings you take walks through the surrounding pine forests, sometimes swimming laps in a small pond that you discovered. When in need of groceries, you hike to your car at the trailhead and drive into N——, but otherwise you allow yourself to luxuriate in the seclusion of the cabin. Whole days pass without your seeing or hearing another human being. The advertisement was vague on the question of your duties: you are only to *maintain the general upkeep*. Really, the post sounded like a sinecure. And because the *general upkeep*, judging by the state of the lawn, does not need much maintaining, you do not bother tending the property. The one morning you try to, you get no further than searching for equipment. All you can find is a supply shed at the edge of the backyard, a small shack of corrugated tin, with nothing inside that could be of any use to you: an empty tool chest, a cord of firewood, some wattle fencing. And leaning against the side of the shed, a rusted push mower.

Only at night are you reminded that the man is sick. During the day you are able to put it out of your consciousness entirely. But, lying on his mattress, waiting to fall asleep, you stare at the dreamcatcher in the bedroom window and think of every mad thought that has authored it. Each night your last waking thoughts are of the owner and his nightmares, so much so that you half expect to have one yourself. In the mornings you are even mildly surprised to discover that you haven't. The whole first week in the cabin, your dreams are untroubled and blank, utterly unmemorable mere moments after waking. Perhaps, you catch yourself thinking, the dreamcatchers are working.

Then, on the final evening of that initial week, you suffer what you think of as a waking nightmare. It happens while you are staring at yourself in the owner's bathroom mirror, getting ready for bed. This is the first time you have really studied your reflection here, and you are struck by the dirtiness of the glass, the way it is covered with thin streaks of grime. The bathroom is closet-sized and, except for the brick of glass in the shower stall, windowless. Behind your reflection in the mirror, you can see the moldy vinyl of the shower's yellow curtain, and behind that, you know, is the brick-shaped window's dreamcatcher. Examining the streaks in the mirror, you notice that they, too, form a kind of dreamcatcher: a system of threads crisscrossing its surface in a network.

The streaks are whitish with furrows down the middle, like the contrails of jets. You had assumed at first that they were grime—some naturally occurring buildup or encrustation of mildew—in which case their reticulation would be incidental. But the longer you look at them, the more you convince yourself that they form a deliberate pattern. The lines are too finely controlled to be random. They cut across the mirror in wide crescents, in sustained curves and careful arcs that, occasionally intersecting, overlap in Borromean rings. Every line is a line of intent. Even here, in the bathroom's mirror, the owner has installed a dreamcatcher! You cannot help imagining how he drew it: leaning over the porcelain sink with a pink wedge of eraser, pressing one corner of the rubber to the mirror and dragging. You picture the owner tracing an entire dreamcatcher in this way, inscribing its protective pattern on the glass.

You try centering your face inside the dreamcatcher's streaks, until their network is superimposed over you like a wire cage. You stare into your snared reflection. The garish bathroom light makes your eyes seem more sunken and your cheekbones sharper than they are. Transverse streaks cut across your cheeks, your forehead, and your chin, introducing distortions into the reflection. Beneath the streaks your flesh turns the translucent color of flesh behind frosted glass. These arcs of blur seem to mar your skin like scar tissue. The meshwork is totally flat, laid over your face in a two-dimensional grid. But you find that if you focus your eyes on some fixed point—allowing your peripheral vision to soften and letting your reflection merge with the meshwork—it really does look as if the streaks are bending to wrap around your face. They seem to drape over it, like a net.

You focus on your eyes. You look into them until they begin to look back at you, and your face grows estranged in this way. Soon you cease to recognize your own reflection. It looks like a stranger's face: the sunken eyes, the sharp cheekbones. Deep down, you know that it is your face. But the more intently you stare at it, the less yourself it seems, for it keeps staring intently back at you. In the muscles of your face—in the sensation of the skin on your cheeks and forehead—you feel your expression to be one of focused concentration and scrutiny. Except this is not the expression that the stranger has on its face. Seeing your so-called concentration and scrutiny reflected in its face, you would swear that it is an expression of tranquil hatred. The face in the mirror regards you with quiet, simmering intensity, the sunken eyes murderous above the sharp cheekbones. It looks as if it wants to kill you. It looks as if it is fantasizing about it right now. And the more frightened that this makes you—the more fearful you feel your own face becoming—the more hateful grows the expression on its face. Its hatred seems to grow in direct proportion to your fear. You even feel a paradoxical fear of becoming any more afraid, a panicked need to stop being afraid *this instant*: not only because your fear is irrational—the face is merely a reflection—but also because you want to staunch the strengthening hatred of its face. Yet you cannot help growing afraid: your fear only mounts, and with it, the hatred, and with it, more fear. When you feel the blood draining from your own face, the reflection's face grows pale, as with rage. And when this makes you short of breath, the reflection's face tightens, as with rage. And when at this your own eyes dry and widen, the look in the reflection's eyes is like a nightmare you are having.

Unable any longer to bear the pressure of its gaze, you flinch. You glance away from the mirror and toward the bathroom wall, where, at just this moment, an apricot-colored spider is emerging from behind the right-hand side of the mirror's frame. It crawls slowly into view, its orange body grotesque against the raw logs. You realize that it must live there, behind the mirror, in that dark centimeter of space. It crawls in a jerky, stop-motion way that is terrible to watch. Its body is coin-sized and finely jointed and where the garish bathroom light catches in its hollow legs, flooding them with warm amber, they look like straws of honey. The fact that the spider *lives behind the mirror* strikes you as unnatural and unnerving. It lives behind the mirror the way monsters live beneath beds.

Soon the sight of the spider becomes less bearable to you than the memory of your reflection, and you return your attention to the mirror. There the reflection is, still enmeshed in the intersecting streak marks. Remarkably, the face has remained estranged. It is still an other's face. But now the meshwork of blurred lines resembles a spiderweb, not a dreamcatcher. And you cannot help picturing the spider that has spun it: this sinister spider emerging from behind the mirror at night to crawl across the mirror's surface, dragging one back leg behind it to streak the glass. You imagine the spider tracing an entire web this way, its apricot body moving over the mirror in the great loops and curves it is used to—instinctively reproducing, with its leg, the pattern programmed into its very being.

You are certain that the apricot spider is responsible for these streaks. It has woven this web of misrecognition in the mirror: where faces get stuck in its threads like flies, they can no longer be recognized. A face is caught in it right now. It is not your face. And before you can witness the spider clambering onto the mirror to begin feeding on this face, you flee the bathroom.

In the bare light of the next morning you return to find that the mirror's streaks do not look like anything anymore. You can discern no organizing design in them—just a random arrangement of stray lines. With a wet paper towel you wipe away the grime. When you have finished, you lift the mirror a few inches off the wall, leaning around to peer behind it. But of course there is no trace of the apricot spider. It was foolish, you tell yourself, to let yourself get whipped into such a frenzy last night. Scared of your own reflection! You resolve to spend the day swimming laps in the pond. You need to get out of the house. For the space of an hour, it seems, you thought the kinds of thoughts the owner would think, and believed in the superstitions that he believes. As if you were contracting not cabin fever, but the owner's very madness.

A month passes in routine. You go into N— less and less: just once every week or so, to stock up on groceries. You also leave the cabin less frequently, find yourself growing used to it. While you still take hikes through the forest to the little pond in the mornings, there are some afternoons when you do not leave at all. You forget about the owner and his nightmares; you become so acclimated to the dreamcatchers that you learn to ignore the sight of them. Indeed, you can go days at a time without remembering that the owner even exists, that the cabin, the forests, and the pond are not your own personal property.

And then one morning, while exploring the backyard, you discover the silhouettes. In the month that you have neglected it, the yard has grown thicker and taller with weeds. This morning the sky is clear and the sun high, but a mist has not yet burned off the mountain, so the tall grasses clump wetly together. You have to force your way forward, pushing with your hip, to penetrate the overgrowth. But once you reach the middle of the yard, the grass gives way suddenly: you stumble onto a small clearing, an elliptical enclosure measuring about two dozen feet. The owner must have mowed it before he left. It is on the ground of this clearing that you see the silhouettes: six black blotches spanning the width of the enclosure, evenly spaced and placed side by side, as dark against the green grass as char marks. You even take them for char marks, at first, scorches from an electrical storm. Then you notice their vaguely human shapes, the regularity in the row of them. Clearly these are silhouettes that the owner has made. Crouching to inspect one, you see that the blackened blades are indeed glossy and stiff, as with paint, and that your own shadow, compact and hunched inside itself, fills in the blotch's outline perfectly. Scanning the perimeter of the enclosure, you spot the discarded can of spray paint, half buried by the rim of weeds, its cylinder's cap jet-black. The six shapes look like crows perched along a power line, or like the chalked outlines of murdered men.

As for what the owner must have been thinking while he made them, you cannot fathom. The silhouettes seem no less insane than the dreamcatchers. On the one hand, there is the ritual installation of the dreamcatchers; and on the other hand, the ritual effigiation of the silhouettes. On the one hand, *hammering into place all the dreamcatchers*; and on the other hand, *painstakingly stenciling these silhouettes*. It is likely that the two rituals are interrelated: that both the dreamcatchers and the silhouettes are involved, somehow, in his idée fixe about nightmares. The only question is what role the latter plays. Like the dreamcatchers, the silhouettes probably constitute one more line of defense in the prophylactic apparatus of the cabin. Anthropomorphic, minatory, what they most resemble are scarecrows. Would the owner have thought they could ward off flocks of nightmares, established in the yard like this? You would not put it past him. Though it is possible that he had some other, more insane plan for them altogether.

You stare at the six dark blotches on the grass, pretending they form an elaborate Rorschach test. To arrive at the same interpretation of their pattern as the owner, you must first imagine your way into the particular mythology of his madness. He believes himself to be in a *life or death struggle* with nightmare; he has barricaded his cabin comprehensively against it. At first you assumed that these silhouettes belong to the same defense system. But now you cannot shake the image that the owner, you feel sure, must have of them: anthropomorphic, minatory, what they most resemble are incubi. As if these are the very specters he has boarded himself up against.

Not scarecrows to scare away nightmares, but *nightmares themselves*. Each shadow a hypostatized nightmare. You are certain this is what the owner believes. On those mornings when he woke from a terrible dream, he must have waded out into the clearing with a can of spray paint. By casting his shadow on the ground, he must have imagined he was casting the nightmare from his body. And to complete this unhinged cleansing ritual, he crouched down and filled in the shadow's outline with paint, wrapping the nightmare in black the way a spider wraps its prey in silk. Yes, he would have believed that the blackened ground was itself having a bad dream, coated with the terrors that had coated his mind. Contaminated. To you, of course, the grass blades seem blackened by nothing other than his madness. If they are coated with anything, it is with the thoughts he must have been thinking when he painted them. Moltings of his madness. Part exorcism and part ecdysis.

You reach out your hand toward the foot of one of them, as if to pet its black grasses. But almost immediately you think better of it. For this feels tantamount to plunging your hand into *an anthill of insanity*—your skin coated with the blackness that coats the grass, positively crawling with the thoughts that madden the grass. You snatch back your hand, as from a flame.

But that in itself is a mad thought. It is the kind of thought the owner would think. To prove this point to yourself, you force your fingers forward. You run their tips gingerly over the blackened grass. The blades are stiff and dry.

That night you have trouble falling asleep. You are lying on the owner's mattress in the dark, staring out his bedroom window. You are not afraid of the dreamcatcher there, or of the six silhouettes lying beyond it in the yard. Rather, what unsettles you is the fact that the owner has installed them at all. You keep thinking: you are living in the cabin of a madman. You wonder: how long can you live in a madman's home without going mad yourself?

You are not being superstitious, you do not think. It simply stands to reason. For it would be like sleeping in a house where a family has been slaughtered: whether or not you believe in ghosts, there is the atmosphere to consider. And here, in the cabin of a man who believes himself to be besieged, on every side, by nightmare—the atmosphere is bound to be tinged with insane energies. Before you arrived, the owner was living who knows how long alone between these walls. It is possible that he has polluted the very air with his madness.

You toss about on the mattress and picture the owner lying here, as sleepless as you are. You think of the many nights he must have lain awake, meticulously constructing his mythology. For it *is* meticulous. He has devised rules, and then revised those rules: how the incubi operate and how the dreamcatchers work; what protocols need to be observed when stenciling the silhouettes. Indeed, what in reality he has built is a *thought structure*: hermetic, self-contained, freestanding. This is the house that his madness has constructed around itself; this is the web it has woven. And for who knows how long the owner inhabited it alone, the thought structure's sole occupant: at once its dark architect, seated at the building's center, and its dark spider, patiently spinning out its thread. Now that he is gone, this center is empty, but the vacant thought structure remains. Oblivious, you have wandered right inside it, like a visitor to the house, or, yes—why not say it?—like a fly into a web.

It seems unlikely that the owner was always mad. You doubt, for instance, that he arrived at the cabin and began installing dreamcatchers first thing, initiating the silhouette ritual first thing. Probably, he was mildly paranoid when he first retired here, and only after prolonged seclusion did his delusions worsen. For that matter, he may even have been perfectly sane when he arrived. Prolonged seclusion would warp even a perfectly sane person's thought processes eventually. That is the nature of cabin fever: the isolation gets to you in its own good time. If the cabin does not drive you straight out of your mind—if you absolutely refuse to be driven out of your mind—very well: then the cabin will find a way of driving itself straight *into* your mind, implanting an insanity there itself. The insanity is simply a nail, but the cabin is the hammer.

And now here you are, alone not only inside the cabin, which hammers at you with cabin fever, but also inside the owner's thought structure, which hammers at you with madness. The prudent thing would be to take your half of the stipend and abandon the position immediately. Already you are showing signs of strain, after all: that midnight access of irrationality at the mirror. But then again, on the other hand, there are only two months remaining. You can withstand two months. Two months is not nearly enough time for you to be driven mad. Now if you had to stay six months, maybe, a year. But two months?

You turn over in bed and stare at the ceiling. Your mind is racing. You cannot stop analyzing the relationship between architecture and psychology. Even at the etymological level, your mind cannot stop cataloguing all the terms that the vocabularies of architecture and psychology share. *Entrance*, for example. For while *entrance* is a psychological verb, referring to the process of hypnosis, it is also, at the same time, an architectural noun, referring to a point of ingress. To be *entranced*, psychologically, is to be pushed through the *entrance* of an alien thought structure. Hypnotized, you stand inside a new structure of thoughts, one that has been designed especially to encage you. Or the word *threshold*, a noun in both vocabularies. *Threshold* refers—psychologically—to liminality, the spaces between perceptual awareness. And yet *threshold* also refers—architecturally—to the doorways that separate distinct rooms. The thoughts you think in the bathroom differ qualitatively from the thoughts you think in the hall, and dividing these thought systems—no less than the physical spaces themselves—is a threshold. When you cross a threshold, psychologically, you are passing from one room of thought into another.

You wonder whether such a *structure of thought*—which, like any structure, also has its entrances and its thresholds—might ever actually become coextensive with a building: whether it would be possible for a thought structure and a physical structure to overlap. If an occupant lives a long enough time alone in the same building, and if his mental layout is gradually scaffolded over the rooms in which he thinks—then yes, you decide, eventually the two structures will grow concentric. If you step over the threshold of that building, you pass over the threshold into its thoughts. Crossing the entrance of that building, you are entranced. And if the thought structure happens to be a mad one, then you must move from room to room in that madness.

You really are living inside a madman's thought structure, you realize, and his madness's mansion has many rooms. In a spasm, you clutch at the bedsheets with your fingers. Your brain is racked by a black panic. Sitting up, you survey the empty room around you. It seems to reel, spinning as if you were drunk. Beneath the baseboards, behind the joists, you can visualize— as in an X-ray—a cage of translucent gray lines, shadowed like bone. And when your temples throb, you can feel the room driving itself into your mind. You can feel the cabin and its thought structure hammering away, driving itself deeper inside. It will go on pounding for as long as it takes, you know, until finally you internalize it, introjecting all the owner's psychical architecture. Then your mind will mimic the layout of that madman's mind completely. Like two apartments in a complex, your mind and the owner's mind, mirror images of each other: two insanities sharing a floor plan.

Gritting your teeth, you clench your eyes violently, as if trying to crush something between cheek and brow. What you are trying to crush is every throbbing thought in your skull.

In the morning you take a walk through the backyard, cutting a wide berth around the field's middle. You have not slept all night.

It is a cool morning, dim with impending sunrise. For a while you are able to admire the dawn. Lying on a slope just three hundred feet beneath the timberline, the backyard commands an eastern prospect of declivitous pine grove and horizon, and, staring ahead, you can see clear out across the forests. The woods stretch forever away and down, black avalanche bristling the foothills. Above the dark margin of the lower fir forests is an argent margin of overcast, and at the border dividing them is a thin interstice of gold light. You listen as a breeze insufflates the pine trees. Even at this distance you can hear it, a hissing like water sizzling all over the mountain. You turn to head back toward the cabin, and at this moment a strong wind blows, giving the pines to sough again. Suddenly the sound is hateful to you. For now that hiss reminds you not of water sizzling, but of the noise a threatened spider makes: a circumambient, mandibular sound, sibilant, as if the entire mountain is hissing in your ear. The wind picks up, and the hissing intensifies. It engulfs you. You hurry back to the cabin to escape the wind, and as you walk you keep your eyes fixed on the porch and your hands cupped tightly over your ears.

The following day you sit at the dining room table with a sheet of paper and a pen. At the sheet's heading, you scrawl the word HOUSESITTING, and beside it, the various positions that this encompasses: GUARDIAN, CUSTODIAN, SENTRY. None describe your function in the cabin. You are no longer sure what that function is. And lately a troubling thought has occurred to you. It is an obvious thought, yet only now do you think it: it is that you, too—*the house sitter*—must be playing some role in the owner's thought structure. Like the dreamcatchers, like the silhouettes, you must figure somehow into his madness.

You meet no practical need by being here. Aside from the dreamcatchers, there is nothing to protect in this place, no property to guard. Some furniture, the contents of the toolshed—nothing, or close to nothing. Nor is there any standard of *general upkeep* to maintain. The place needs no house sitter, yet the owner has hired a house sitter. It follows that he must have had a unique conception of house-sitting. If the typical duties or responsibilities do not apply to the cabin, then the owner must have had in mind different duties—no doubt madder duties, *more frightful ones.*

Does he expect you to clean out the dreamcatchers each morning? Keep them from clogging? Are you to carry on the ritual of the silhouettes, spray-painting incubi of your own in the enclosure? It is almost as if you have been hired not to house-sit the physical cabin, but to house-sit its parallel thought structure. To occupy and tidy up the owner's thought structure while he is gone.

On the sheet of paper, you study the word *HOUSESITTING.* It is an odd word, you realize. The longer you look at it, the odder it seems. And oddest of all is what the owner could possibly have meant by it. Beneath *HOUSESITTING,* you start a running column of the word's anagrammatic permutations. You begin with *HISSING.* You write the word *GUT,* then the word *SIN.* You write the full sentence *HE IS TO GUT SIN.* Then you superscribe an *E* above the *U* in *GUT,* so that the sentence optionally reads *HE IS TO GET SIN.* You notice you can make *NOUS.* Below, you write the full sentence *I GET THIS NOUS.* You can feel yourself closing in on something here. You are sure that the true nature of *house-sitting,* what it really is and means, is hidden somewhere inside *HOUSESITTING.* When the owner placed an advertisement for a *house sitter,* it was really this hidden something that he was soliciting. And you can just see it, embedded in the letters, catching your eye and calling out to you to be deciphered: a secret meaning that, if only you could crack its code, would illuminate everything. You keep rearranging the twelve letters into short, complete sentences. *H... I GUESS IT NOT,* you write.

You write the word *HOST.* Below, you write the words *GUEST* and, beside it in the margin, *GEIST.* Then, in an inspired and almost automatic way, you find yourself writing, *I UNGHOST SITE*. You set the pen down on the table and stare at this sentence. You feel sure that this is it. What is more, you are certain that *ghost* in particular is the one word you have this whole time been searching for: the hidden element that has been haunting *HOUSESITTING* from within, *catching your eye* and *calling out to you*; the pea buried beneath all of *HOUSESITTING*'s anagrammatic mattresses, giving the word no rest.

The owner has brought you here to unghost the site. You picture the silhouettes lying in the backyard enclosure: each hypostatized nightmare is a human shape, a *shade*. It is easy to believe that the owner believes that these incubi are like so many ghosts, haunting him and the cabin. And even that they might discover some way, in his absence, of infiltrating the cabin: that he would return to find the building infested with specters, overrun by them, the logs riddled with nightmares as with termites. There is no question why he would hire a house sitter under such circumstances. He would need someone here to perform an exorcistic function. That, then, is the role that you have been assigned. You are to *unghost* the site by occupying it, to repel these specters by your presence. The house sitter is literally to *sit* in the house, in the same way and for the same reasons that you would sit in another's chair while they were gone: to prevent strangers from taking it, to keep it warm. That is, precisely, to keep *cold spots* from developing in it.

But an alternate interpretation of *I UNGHOST SITE* also occurs to you, an uglier interpretation, and one that is even easier to believe. Namely, that you are to unghost the owner's ghosts in the same way that you are to introject his thought structure: by inheriting them. That the madman intends to offer you up as a sacrifice to these shades, some substitute or scapegoat to be haunted in his place. He would have the silhouettes torment you rather than him; he would have them drive you mad until they drive you off the mountain, and not only that, but drive themselves right inside you as well, into your mind, so that you take them away with you when you leave. Out of sheer spite you ball up the sheet of paper and throw it onto the floor. So, you think. He thinks you will be the herd of swine into which his Legion can be driven, then be driven off the mountain. He thinks his nightmares will drive themselves right inside you, then drive the both of you straight off the mountain. Well, he will find that you are not so docile as a herd of swine. You step on the balled-up paper and grind it beneath your heel until the dining room resounds with the dry-leaf sound of its crepitating.

The mountain contains the forest; the forest contains the weed field; the weed field contains the enclosure, which contains the shadows, and it also contains the cabin, which is coextensive with the thought structure; the cabin and the thought structure both contain the dining room, whose walls contain the table at which you are sitting. Each container smaller than the last, and embedded inside it, like a series of nested parentheses. And at the center of this series is you. Every layer presses inward to where you sit. The mechanism is trying to crush your mind from all sides. But you are not worried, because *you will never be driven mad.* You sit calmly in the smallest chamber of all, your skull, impervious to the currents rippling against you: wall, wall, shadow, field. You are the one sane sentence at the heart of the parenthetical. You cannot be erased.

By midnight you can no longer endure staying inside the cabin. You pace from room to room. You can see now all the ways in which the owner is trying to drive you mad. You see how the cabin has been laid for you like a trap.

There is no question that the rooms have been scrupulously arranged to make you lose your mind: the dreamcatchers in the windows, the bareness of the walls, even the placement of the furniture—it is all rich with significance. Each detail is specifically designed to catch your attention and invite interpretation. You are meant to wonder what the owner must have been thinking when he arranged these things and, in this manner, to think your way into the owner's thoughts.

For instance, that chair in the living room. Tonight you notice, as if for the first time, how strange it is that one chair has been removed from the coffee table in the room's center and positioned in the northeast corner. The three other chairs remain around the coffee table, identical to one another and to the missing chair: beige, unpainted, the wood of their railings splintered. But the fourth chair has been conspicuously set apart from the others. Its seat faces the corner, opposite the vertical crease where the northern and eastern walls meet, with its scalloped back to the room, such that anyone seated in it would see nothing but wall. The chair is positioned like the stool of a dunce.

Why would the owner position a chair like the stool of a dunce? What would have possessed him, not only to remove the chair from the coffee table, but also to set it in this eccentric position? He must have needed the extra elevation of the chair's seat, perhaps standing on it to replace a lightbulb. Except that *there is no light socket above the chair.* The only light in the room is the bare bulb dangling from an exposed wire above the coffee table. No, if the owner had decided impulsively to move the chair, it must have been motivated—like everything else—by his madness. The chair, too, you realize—*even the chair*—must be playing some role in his thought structure.

What must the owner have been thinking? What thoughts must have been passing through his mind? But this thought, you understand, is exactly what the chair *wants* you to think! The chair has been placed in the corner for no other reason than to elicit this thought in you. And that, that exactly, is what you loathe about the chair: that it coerces you into wondering *what the owner must have been thinking*, that it forces you to imagine all the thoughts passing through that madman's mind. Now you cannot help thinking his thoughts. *I should like to punish my nightmare*, the owner must have thought, you think. *I should like to banish my nightmare to the corner. I will make it sit in time-out, facing the wall.* He must have hallucinated one of his own nightmares sitting in that chair: a paper-thin silhouette or incubus, facing the corner like a dunce. The man is absolutely mad!

You can no longer even bear it, staring at the chair. The sight of it there in the corner forces you to reconstruct the line of the madman's reasoning. And to think the thoughts that a madman must have thought is, you know, only another way of going mad. It would not be an exaggeration to say that when you think the thoughts that the owner must have thought, the owner is thereby invading your mind. He is possessing you via these thoughts about the chair—*he is haunting the chair*. Indeed, if the cabin is haunted by anything, it is not by ghosts of the owner's nightmares—it is by ghosts of the owner's madness. You can sense, sitting invisibly in the chair, all the thoughts that the owner must have thought about it. They haunt the chair. You, in turn, are haunted by that chair.

You stare at the chair. If you were ever to actually sit in it, you know, oh, it would be just like sitting in an electric chair: the owner's thoughts would course into your body, flowing through you in currents. Your body would absolutely surge with the owner's thoughts. They would be all that you could ever think.

You do not sleep that night. At first light of morning you stalk to the edge of the backyard to retrieve the push mower. The owner wants you to unghost the site? You will show him exactly how you go about unghosting sites.

You find the push mower still leaning against the side of the toolshed. A rusted contraption not much larger than a vacuum cleaner, it must have been left out in all weather: the red paint of its chassis is chipping badly, and the tips of its blades—lining the denticulate cylinder in its casing—are dull. It barely cuts grass anymore. You test it on the fringe of weeds where it stands, which rise as high as halfway up its steel handlebar. Setting the mower down in a patch and gripping that handlebar, you struggle for fifteen minutes, ramming the chassis back and forth over the grass stems. Each glossy green stalk just spools itself around the rotating cylinder, catching between its blades like floss. This causes the mower to halt, and you have to shove on it to uproot the recalcitrant grasses. Only then—after making multiple passes over that same fringe of weeds—can you effortfully shred them to confetti. It takes you half a dozen passes. When you are finished, the tendons in your arms burn with strain. Your skin is covered in a fine sheen of sweat and plastered over with little green flecks of grass shrapnel.

It will take entirely too long to trim the yard this way. You simply carry the mower to the enclosure in the middle. If nothing else, you will mow the silhouettes. Now you stand over the leftmost shadow, the chassis positioned atop its feet. You should be able to make quick work of them all. Their grass blades, already trimmed once by the owner, are shorter and more manageable, and probably brittle from the paint.

Starting from the bottom, you work your way up the shadow's body. The mower practically glides over the ground. Its rotating cylinder rakes its blades through the legs, torso, head, meeting little resistance from the bristly grass. The soil churns up in friable clods. And as the mower masticates the shadow, it spits out bits of it backward, strewing a trail of the silhouette's confetti. Whatever the silhouette is, the mower pulverizes it. If it is a hypostatized nightmare, then the mower is shredding that nightmare. And if it is a hypostatized madness, then the mower is shredding that madness. This morning, however, you think of the silhouettes neither as hypostatized nightmares nor as madnesses. You think of them as load-bearing columns in the owner's thought structure: if you demolish them, it will collapse.

You mow the first silhouette in just two passes, once forward and once back. What is left in its place is a piebald pile of green and black grass blades. To the pile's right, the five remaining silhouettes patiently await their fates. Together, they really do resemble prey in a spider's web: wrapped tight in their cocoons of silk, in these black shrouds of spray paint. Incubus husks. You ready the mower to unghost them.

After returning the push mower to its place beside the tool-shed, you spend the rest of the morning tearing down the dreamcatchers and packing your duffel bag. You pack the dreamcatchers, too. You have decided to take your half of the stipend and leave first thing tomorrow. As for the other half, your compensation will just have to be imagining the look on the owner's face: the expression he will have on entering the cabin, when he realizes not only that you have not been driven mad but also that you have mercilessly—and, indeed, perfectly sanely—dismantled his prophylactic apparatus, stripping the windowpanes and trimming the silhouettes.

Now it is night, your last in the cabin, and you have been standing at the bedroom window, staring out at the backyard. Beyond the pane, the grass merges into a single sealike mass, and all that can be distinguished in the darkness is the far figure of the toolshed: a shack of corrugated tin lit up by the orange haze of its safety lamp, the push mower visible in silhouette. The only object in the frame, the shed is what you have been focusing on tonight, and what you imagine the owner must have focused on, too, those nights when he stood here staring out the window. The shed stands at the edge of the yard, appearing in the lower left-hand corner of the windowpane. Its roof slants over the entryway in a slight lip, sheltering it, and affixed to this soffit is the safety lamp: a single bulb burning in a casing of translucent plastic. The casing casts a widening cone of rust-toned light before the shed, washing it a granular red. Because the shed emerges from the black grasses and from the window frame stained this blood-orange color, it recalls the horizon rutilance of a rising moon. In the sky tonight there is no moon. The only source of light is the shed itself, glowing alone in the broader darkness.

There is something eerie about the quality of that lamplight. How thin it is and full of shadows, like the lighting of a long hallway in a dream. You can see where the doorless entryway to the shed gapes black. The lamp hangs directly above it, casting its cone of light downward: there the grainy haze creates a nightmare space, a space of expectancy. If it were the owner standing here tonight, he would almost certainly be waiting for something to step out into that cone of light. He would be bracing himself to see something emerge from the shed. And every second that something did not exit the shed and enter the cone of light, it would only become more certain, and more dreadful, that some vague, dark shape was about to exit the toolshed and enter the light.

Then there actually is the vague, dark shape to consider: the push mower. Leaning against the toolshed where you left it, just inside that cone of light, even the push mower takes on a sinister aspect. At this distance, its silhouette is easily mistaken for a man's, for example. Whole seconds at a time, you can convince yourself that it is not a push mower at all. This is surely what the owner would be convincing *him*self, you understand. Even as he recognized, deep down, that the silhouette is merely the push mower, he would see in it nevertheless a man's shape. He would convince himself that it is not just any silhouette, but one of *his* silhouettes: one of the backyard shadows risen from the ground of the enclosure. Staring longer and longer at its vague, dark shape, there in the grainy haze of the cone of light, he would whip himself into a frenzy, convincing himself of everything that the silhouette is: not a push mower, but an incubus, stock-still before the toolshed. Something malevolent, staring back at him. Looking straight through the bedroom window.

At this thought the owner would—as an hour ago you did—turn off the bedroom's light, so that he could peer surreptitiously through the darkened pane. And invisible now he would—as all night you have been doing—stand sentry at the window.

The safety lamp's bulb does not burn constantly. Activated by a timer, it burns for fifteen minutes and then blinks out, to prevent overheating. In this way, the shed gets bathed in its orange aureole only for quarter-hour intervals. Then, whenever the bulb blinks out, the shed is plunged into a vanishing darkness. Right now, for instance—even as you watch—the bulb snaps off, causing the shed to disappear. The windowpane goes instantly flat and black, and for a moment you see nothing. Your eyes adjust slowly, until you can descry the outline of the shed: a frame of slightly purer darkness carved into the night, like a trapdoor of blackness. Glowing faintly inside this outline is the safety lamp's casing. Although the bulb is off, you can still make out an orange remnant where its coils cool. You see it suspended in the emptiness of the blackened windowpane, a wisp of ember. You can no longer distinguish the push mower at all.

It takes seven minutes for the coils to finish cooling and warm back up again. You have watched the lamp reignite approximately a dozen times tonight. The buildup leading to its combustion is always a minor drama. As the coils warm, the wisp of ember expands, so gradually that you barely notice. Its orange core keeps on thickening in diameter, pushing out through the plastic casing, until every inch of it is filled. Before the lamp snaps back on, the casing simply smolders there awhile, a red-hot block in the blackness. It looks like a brick being baked in midnight's kiln. It throbs orange. Then, just as unexpectedly as it snapped off, the bulb reignites. A starburst explodes outward from the lamp, sharp spokes of light that asterisk the air.

Every time the lamp combusts like this, the push mower's silhouette is thrown into relief, a jag of shadow beside the shed entrance. All night it has not moved. Now, if you were the owner, and if you believed that that silhouette actually was an incubus, and if hour after hour you watched the lamp flash on to reveal that it had not budged, you would find this tremendously unsettling. Not only that the silhouette has not changed positions but also that, during the fifteen-minute intervals when it is lit, the silhouette does not even flinch. It does not so much as turn its head or shift its weight to a different leg. With a statue's poise, or a push mower's, it remains fixed there, inhuman and unmoving.

That is what would unsettle you about the silhouette, if you were the owner: the lengths to which it is willing to go to convince you that it is a push mower. How it stands precisely in the push mower's place. How it keeps its arms folded at its sides and its legs pressed together, the better to simulate the push mower's shape. How it will go on standing there as still, and for as long, as it takes to be mistaken for an inanimate object, and how only then—when you have finally mistaken it for a push mower and reassured yourself, *After all, it is only the push mower*—only when you have turned your back on the so-called push mower and abandoned your vigil before the bedroom window, how only then will the silhouette, taking advantage of your negligence, reveal itself for what it truly is: from the straight black line it makes, its arms will unfold liquidly at its sides, and the lower half of the silhouette's body scissor apart into two dark legs. This, *this*, is what unsettles you: how in one second, after hours of ruthless patience, the silhouette will finally transform itself, shifting from a push mower into a man.

There *is* something unsettling about the sight of it, when the lamp is lit. A dark shape in an orange haze. It really does look human. It really does look as if it is looking back at you, right through the bedroom window. And even more unsettling than this, you find, are those periodic seven-minute intervals—such as now—when the lamp is *not* lit. For then the silhouette merges completely with the darkness, and you cannot see it. During this time, for all you know, it could be anywhere: not in its usual position beside the entryway, but halfway across the yard, lurching toward the cabin. While you have kept your eyes trained on the toolshed's outline—as you do now—waiting impatiently for the safety lamp to reignite, the incubus could already be cutting across the weeds. Then, when the lamp finally does flash on, you might see only the awful emptiness of that cone of light, untenanted at last. For if suddenly, for the first time in hours, the cone of light were empty? Then you would know for certain. You would know—*beyond a shadow of a doubt*—that it is not and never has been a push mower, that it has always been a nightmare, merely biding its time. And at the sight of the vacant cone your mind would jam with panic, trying to calculate where, by now, this incubus could be.

Right now, as it so happens, only a minute remains before the lamp flashes back on. And if the silhouette is not there? You reject this thought out of hand. It is impossible. The silhouette cannot be one of the enclosure's shadows, because you have mowed the enclosure's shadows. Not the shadow, but the mower that has masticated the shadow: that is the only thing the silhouette could be.

Of course, if you were the owner, you might find ways of believing otherwise. Say, for instance, that by mowing the shadows you have simply freed them: that you liberated each nightmare from the cage that the thought structure made around it, or the cocoon that the spray paint made around it. If you were the owner, you might grow to rue right now, with ramping horror, the magnitude of your error. For you have accomplished nothing, or worse than nothing, by mowing the black shadows, you would think. You have simply unleashed their nightmares, disseminating their energies freely. So far from unghosting the site, you have *unleashed the very ghosts upon the site*. This is the thought that would cause you to bite the inside of your cheek right now, until it bled, and pound on your thigh with a panicked fist, internally cursing the lamplight to hurry, if you were the owner and thought as the owner thinks, and if you believed what he believes about the silhouette. If you believed every last thing that madman believes.

In the darkness of the yard, hanging inside the toolshed's darker outline, the casing of the safety lamp is radiating orange warmth like a baking brick. If you were the owner, you would not be able to pry your eyes away. Because you would *know* what that cone of light is about to reveal: no silhouette beside the entryway, only a heart-stopping emptiness. For deep down you would also know—*beyond a shadow of a doubt*—that it is not and never was a push mower. It is a nightmare, and you have freed it. When the lamp flashes on, you will see this. The lamp flashes on.

The Bookcase

1.

FROM WBEZ CHICAGO IT'S *THIS AMERICAN LIFE*, distributed by Public Radio International. I'm Ira Glass. Every week on our show of course we choose a *theme*, bring you different kinds of stories *on* that theme, and this week that theme is... 'Over My Dead Body.' Stories of regular people who want something *so much*, want one particular thing so *badly*... that they're willing to fight to the death for it. Our show in four acts today, each of which starts with a thing and ends in a showdown for possession of that thing. Act 1, 'The Will To Power': in this act a family is torn apart by strange provisions in their parents' will, devised as a practical joke from beyond the grave. Act 2, 'Citation Needed': how one writer decides to *sit vigil* over his Wikipedia page, once anonymous users begin revising it. Act 3, 'Partially Furnished': what happens when you have to fight your landlady, really physically *fight* her, for a piece of furniture that you both know is yours. Act 4, 'The Magic Matzo': a new short story from *This American Life* contributor Etgar Keret, about a very special dumpling and the lengths to which people are willing to go to get it. Four desirable objects, four ferocious showdowns—you don't want to miss it. *Stay* with us.

2.

If you've heard episode 529 of *This American Life*, you've heard my voice. I'm Act 3, 'Partially Furnished.' The guy who fought his landlady for a cheap bookcase. I had been telling this story for years before I was invited to tell it on *TAL*. My ex-girlfriend, Michelle, always hated this story.

Her problem, I'd assumed, was simply that she'd heard it too often. The bookcase in question, which had come with me when I moved into her apartment, remained a showpiece in our living room: a six-by-four monument of white particleboard taking up the entire front wall, where the thrift-store eyesore of it—better suited for a dorm than a home—clashed with the rest of her furniture. Whenever friends took a special interest in my books, surveying the spines along its shelves, I liked to share the anecdote. 'I ever tell you how…?' During the time that we were together, Michelle must have endured dozens of performances of this monologue. In the first couple of years she would listen graciously, pretending to laugh along with the guests. But eventually I would catch her rolling her eyes when I began, subtly excusing herself to use the bathroom. 'They only have to hear the story,' she told me once. 'I have to live with it.' Finally one night, as we were lying in bed after a party, she started to recite my monologue back to me. I had told it so frequently in the past five years, she claimed, that nothing in the narrative was fluid or improvisatory. Each detail, each transition, and each beat had long since ossified into its final form, a script that she could deliver herself if she had to: 'This was the summer after college'; 'All it lacked was a bookcase.' In the dark of our bedroom, I felt my face growing hot with self-consciousness, though she wasn't being spiteful or unfair. It really was my favorite story.

Then, one morning last year, the call came from Chicago. An intern explained that an old acquaintance of ours, Carleen, was now working at WBEZ, where she happened to be present when *TAL* producers were pitching ideas for the upcoming 'Over My Dead Body' episode. Carleen had mentioned my bookcase story, and Ira had just loved it. He would be in town the following weekend and wanted to meet to record a quick segment. Flustered, and flattered, I agreed. The intern would email the details.

When I told Michelle the news, she didn't even attempt a smile. 'And you're going to do it?' she asked. 'You're going to appear on the show?' I said of course, and she said that was great. But she said it in that flat, trapped voice hostages have, when someone with a gun at their back is telling them to say everything's great. So it came as no surprise that afternoon when she suggested we have a talk.

After dinner she walked me through her misgivings regarding the interview. We were sitting in the living room. She'd taken her place, cross-legged, on the sofa; I was on the ottoman opposite, with the bookcase behind me. Her misgivings involved three 'prongs,' she explained, mischievously. She was using the word to needle me, I knew: academic rhetoric she'd picked up presenting conference papers. She asked me not to interrupt, not until she'd finished with all three of them, then reassured me that this was nothing serious, just something she needed to get off her mind. On the glass-topped coffee table between us she'd set down two tumblers of whiskey, a ritual she'd developed for alleviating difficult discussions.

The first prong was that it was a nasty story. 'You bullied an old woman and stole her bookcase,' she said. I must have flinched, for she added, '—is one way of looking at it.' I nodded for her to continue. 'In your shoes,' she pressed on, 'someone else might be ashamed. But there isn't a friend of ours you haven't bragged to about your exploits. And casting yourself as the hero every time, playing up her age and playing it for laughs.' In our mid-twenties this had seemed charming, she said, but now that I was thirty, and the story hadn't matured at all, she could no longer ignore the callousness in my treatment of Fredricka. And who knew what our friends were thinking? The way I gloated over this poor, lonely woman, as if she were a cartoon, as if she had it coming to her. 'Consider it from her point of view. How do you think she tells the story to *her* friends?' Fredricka did not have any friends, though I resisted the temptation to say so. Michelle gestured to the space beside the sofa, as if insinuating a scene, and I realized that she was waiting for me to imagine the woman telling the story to her friends. I stared into the space, taking a sip of whiskey, and visualized three blue-haired ladies sitting around Fredricka, covering their mouths in polite gapes of horror. I said I supposed I'd look like the bad guy, from her point of view. 'Right,' Michelle said. 'Like a thief and a bully. A tormentor. Antagonizing her.' Even without the proviso against interjecting mid-prong, I knew this would have been a bad time to correct her, for instance by noting that I could not have been a 'thief,' since the bookcase was rightfully mine, or that Fredricka had been the one who bullied and tormented me. That that was the whole point of the story. I took another, larger sip from my tumbler, inhaling deeply before I drank: the bouquet was strong, and the bourbon burned. I nodded again for her to go on. That was all, she said. For five years she had listened idly by as I regaled everyone with this monologue, and before tonight she'd simply never wanted to be a scold about it.

But now, she said—and this was the second prong—she felt she *had* to say something. Because here I was, about to go on national radio and tell my version of events to a sympathetic host, and not only that, but to a sympathetic audience, which must number into the millions once you account for podcast subscribers. Had I even considered the fact that Fredricka her-self might come to hear it? How did I think she would feel if one day she turned on the radio and heard her bully's voice, blithely narrating one of her most traumatic experiences, all while Ira Glass snickered away? It was one thing to monopolize a narrative in our living room—one thing, among friends, to embellish a story—but...

Here I did have to bite my tongue. It was just like her to accuse me of narrative monopoly, or 'monophony,' as she would call it. Michelle's the kind of angel you can't badmouth anyone around: empathy is a sixth sense with her. If she and her colleagues were sharing departmental gossip, and I joined in by griping about someone stealing my lunch from the office fridge, Michelle would instantly pause. 'Well, we don't know,' she would say, thoughtfully. 'Maybe she had her *reasons* for raiding the refrigerator.' She must have been unusually hungry, for one thing. Had I considered that the woman could be pregnant, diabetic, bulimic, broke? 'Imagine things her way.' One of our earliest fights as a couple, in fact, had been about this habit of hers. Always willing to advocate for the absent party: offering charitable explanations for their behavior; questioning the objectivity of my caricatures; giving voice to the voiceless. And making me seem inconsiderate and cruel in comparison.

I didn't understand why Michelle was so quick to defend people she had never met, or why she trusted their version of events over her boyfriend's. But during that first fight she'd insisted that trust had nothing to do with it. Being a 'polyphonic storyteller' was simply the adult thing to do: if I tried to incorporate other people's perspectives into my own, if I took their motives into consideration and really cultivated a 'dialogic viewpoint,' I would come across as fair and reasonable. 'To your friends, you mean,' I'd said, childishly. She'd sighed.

Michelle folded her arms across her stomach and eased back into the sofa. 'You're not mad?' she asked. I shook my head. The third and final prong, she promised, would sting less—or less personally—than the first two, for it had nothing to do with me. What bothered her most wasn't that I'd agreed to tell this story in a public forum—it was the forum itself. 'We wouldn't even be having this conversation if it were *Judge Judy* you were going on. At least there Fredricka would get her say.' But *TAL* was by its very nature a monophonic institution. *All* its stories were one-sided. Fredricka would not be trotted out from backstage to confront me, and Ira would not challenge my version of events.

It wasn't the show's MO to cross-examine its guests: they were meant to sound like honest, sincere, relatable narrators. This was why all the episodes followed such a rigid formula, according to her. Reporters selected human-interest subjects from the listener demographic—middle-aged, middle-class, usually white—and these 'regular people' proceeded to tell their mildly amusing stories, complaining in wry but soul-searching monologues about their despotic bosses, evil exes, and overbearing parents. The audience identified with them automatically, because they *were* them. And Ira only ever encouraged guests on with his '"heart-felt" voice,' filled with 'spittle and sympathy' for the story they were telling. 'And what better host really, on a show for narrative narcissists,' Michelle asked, 'than *Glass*? He just reflects your own story back to you. Validates your most flattering self-image.' Ira was guaranteed to take my caricature of Fredricka for truth; ditto my rectitude in the bookcase debate. It was up to me what to do with that trust. Either I could abuse it, by vilifying Fredricka as usual and making myself out to be the victim/hero; or I could give a more complicated account of the conflict, detail the moral ambiguity of both our roles. If I didn't speak up for Fredricka, no one would.

She reached toward the coffee table for her tumbler, which had gone untouched throughout her lecture. I had already finished mine and felt warm and calm. I remembered that this was my opportunity to respond: having finished all her 'prongs,' Michelle was waiting to hear what I would have to say about them. She needed to know—needed for me to show her—that I could be mature, sensitive, compassionate: the kind of man she could grow old with. I told her that she was welcome to sit in on the interview, if she wanted. Then I added: 'Of course you'll have heard it all before.' I said: 'I'm just going to tell my story.'

3.

I ever tell you how I got this bookcase? It was for my first apartment. I was living with my landlady at the time, a crabby old woman named Fredricka. This was the summer right after college. I'm talking seventy, maybe eighty years old. She stayed up front, in the master bedroom, and I lived in back, next door to the other boarders: Miranda and Janey, recent grads I rarely saw. Easily the worst landlady I've ever had.

I knew going in, just from the interview, that Fredricka would have preferred not to have to live with me. 'I usually don't rent to *boys*,' is how she put it. This was after she had already led me on a tour of her flat and sat me down in the parlor. She was this withered, scowl-mouthed woman, with crazed white hair and droopy blue eyes. As I read over the lease, she explained that no one else had answered her ad. She was willing to make an exception for *some* boys, of course, but no, quote, 'undesirable types,' which for her meant fraternity brats and trust-fund kids, spoiled children who were used to having maids pick up after them all their lives, and who didn't know how to wash their dishes or sweep their messes. Fredricka hadn't raised *her* son that way. Et cetera. I didn't have a trust fund, or belong to a fraternity, though I doubted these details would have much mattered to her. The clear subtextual caveat of her lecture was, you know, *Danger. Keep Out. Abandon All Hope Ye Brats Who Enter Here.* I smiled as affably as I could. She didn't want to live with me? So she did not want to live with me. She wasn't my ideal roommate, either. The flat smelled like a nursing home, and the creak in her voice—I can't do the creak. *Ye-e-es?* No, I can't. Imagine old vampire movies, that hinge-rich sound when the coffin starts opening. That was her voice. Just unbelievably evil and sour and mean. Yet here we were: I couldn't afford a place of my own, and she couldn't afford to be choosy. Very simply, we did not like each other.

The bedroom itself, though, was perfect, and what's more, it didn't smell so bad with the window open. For a modest month-to-month rent—utilities included—I could have a private space in a beautiful neighborhood, furnished with a bed, dresser, and desk. All it lacked was a bookcase. I requested a rental application and moved in within the week.

At first, there was a grace period between Fredricka and me. It helped that we almost never crossed paths. I spent my free time exploring the neighborhood, and in the flat I mainly lurked in my room. Fredricka, when we did encounter one another, maintained the minimum of civility: how was I liking the neighborhood, the weather—that sort of thing. When I happened to mention that I was in the market for a bookcase, she even said she'd keep an eye out for one.

About the bookcase. Technically, Fredricka was the one who found it. First she checked her storage room in the basement. Nothing. Then, a few days later, she knocked at my door, breathless. I had to come quickly, she said. Her neighbor was dragging his bookcase to the street as trash, and she'd flagged him down for me. Out on the sidewalk, she watched as he and I tried to haul the thing into the building. Shuffling backward up the narrow staircase, peering over the frame, I smiled down at her with what I thought was a grateful expression. But for no reason I could discern, she just glared back at me. Then, tetchily, she hovered behind us as we made our way down the hall. Both times that I scuffed the wallpaper, she gasped theatrically, and once her neighbor had left, she thrust a water spritzer and a washrag at me without a word.

Whatever goodwill had existed between us exploded in that moment. And, ultimately, after four months of mounting acrimony and mutual resentment, I moved. That's the short version. The long version—if you want to bear with me a minute—requires cataloguing at least a few of the small, petty, spiteful things she did to antagonize me.

For one thing, Fredricka was unavoidable. She passed long

days lying in bed in a white nightgown, glowering at the television, waiting for someone to do something she could scold them for. Bedridden, she somehow managed to maintain a panoptic knowledge of all goings-on in the flat, such that if her tenants transgressed any of the hundreds of obsessive details in her lease—by leaving a light on, the faucet dripping, the refrigerator door ajar—the iron-eyed old harridan would crawl out of bed and hobble down to the offender's room, leaving them a mercilessly worded, martinetish Post-it note to find in the morning.

I discovered this for myself about a week after the bookcase incident, when—upon leaving my room—I almost stepped on a plate outside my door. It was one I'd washed and stacked in the drying rack the night before. Squatting down to inspect it, I found a Post-it note stickied to its center: *You missed a spot. –F.* The plate looked spotlessly pink. And then I saw, beside her note, a forensic little thumbprint of grease, which her naked eyes couldn't possibly have been hale enough to see. I picked up the plate and went to the kitchen. She was sitting in wait at the table, and she sucked in her cheeks as I entered. When I apologized, she sneered: 'Don't say you're sorry. Just make sure it doesn't happen again.'

I don't want to bore you—there were dozens of notes like these, I could go on all day. And not just stuck to dishes. One was affixed to an air conditioner, which I'd been running on a sweltering morning, easily in the nineties. That one read: *Crack a window. In the real world, adults have utilities to pay. –F.* Another time, after I'd let my swimsuit drip-dry in the shower, a note slid under my door: *Three other people live in this house. Three other people have to share that bathroom. Don't hang up your* UNDIES *for everyone to see. –F.* Her initial always stung me like a failing grade.

I tried my best not to engage her, but there were limits to what I could bear. For instance, the spoon. She'd placed it at my door, a stray flake of oatmeal barnacled to its stem. Her note read: *If you need help washing dishes, I'd be happy to give you lessons. –F.*

Lessons! The thought of that witch sneaking into the kitchen each night—poring over my dishes in the drying rack, like a schoolteacher searching for typos—filled my throat with blood. On the back of the Post-it, I wrote, *Yes, Fredricka, dishwashing lessons sound lovely. Please let me know your availability.* I left it crumpled on the carpet by her door. By morning it had disappeared.

Three weeks later she found a broken plate in the sink, and things finally came to a head. Her note—arranged with the plate shards outside my room—read simply: *We need to talk. –F.* When I knocked on her door, she called for me to enter, and I saw she was sitting in wait for me, propped up against her bed's headboard in her nightgown—it was three p.m.—and staring at me with queenly severity. I explained that I'd never used the plate, much less broken it, but Fredricka had already deduced that I was the culprit. In gloating tones she walked me through her Sherlockian logic. First, there was the telltale gunk. Who else couldn't wash a dish? Second, Janey and Miranda were, quote, 'mature women' and 'responsible adults,' who could be trusted to confess. Finally, there was my own note, which she produced in a ziplock bag with a dramatic flourish: the third-act scrap of evidence. Really now, a grown man. Asking for *dish*washing lessons. What was she to make of that? As she held the Post-it out for me to see, I realized she must have been preparing this scene since I'd arrived: she the disciplinarian and I the scolded child. I decided then and there that it was time to move. But in meekness, or deference to this feeble old woman sunk into the mattress, I kept my head bent throughout her harangue. Each time she paused to ask some patronizing question—*Did I know* why *we needed to wash our dishes? Had I ever heard of germs?*—I even answered her, in a dutiful monotone, like a student performing his orals: Yes, Fredricka, I had heard of germs. When she was finished, I gave her my one-month's notice, and she smiled a wrinkly, sagging, triumphant smile.

We spent the last few weeks as we had the first, avoiding one another. I boxed up all my books and clothes and moved them to a friend's apartment, leaving the bookcase for a day when I could borrow a truck. However, the weekend before I left I came home to find it—the bookcase—dragged into the hall and lying on its side. Fredricka was waiting for me again in her bedroom. I asked her, you know, what the hell, and she explained that Janey wanted the bookcase now that I was leaving. In a calm voice I told her no, the bookcase wasn't hers to give. She insisted that it was—after all, she was the one who'd found it—and I laughed at her: 'It's street trash! You found it on the street. I'm the one who brought it up the stairs.' To which she screeched: 'My neighbor gave it to *me*! Janey is my tenant, and *I* am giving it to her!' Fine, I said. Janey could have it. But she'd have to wait until I left. I'd paid rent for one last week in what was supposed to be a furnished room—I was almost shouting at this point—and I'd be damned if I was going to let her sneak in while I was gone and haul my furniture away. She couldn't drag my bed out into the hall, so why did she think she could commandeer the bookcase? Fredricka muttered, through literally clenched teeth, that I wasn't even using it. This was true: all my books were already gone, and the shelves were empty. Oh, I assured her, I'd find something to put on it all right. A coffee mug. Socks. Maybe some spare change. The whole week I had left with it, I planned to make the most use of it I could. When I turned to leave, I heard the bedsprings creak, then her creaking voice: 'Don't you dare touch that bookcase! You'll be sorry!'

She followed me down the hall. And when I started to pull the bookcase back into my bedroom, she grabbed the opposite end of it. Still wearing her nightgown, her withered arms straining and shaking, she glowered across at me. I tightened my grip. Honestly, I did not even want the bookcase. Not this much. I just couldn't stand the thought of letting her have it. And somehow, even then, part of me recognized that this moment was more narrative than life—that what was happening, what

I was experiencing, was already material, an anecdote I would be regaling friends with for years: 'That Time I Fought An Old Woman For A Bookcase.' And so I was willing to do almost anything—not just to win the bookcase, but *to make it a better story.* If she wanted a tug-of-war, I was not too proud to give her one.

I planted my feet and heaved the bookcase backward, wrenching it free from her grasp. She scratched at its sides, hobbling after it, trying in vain to reclaim some purchase. After a sloppy lunge, she dropped to the floor, and I froze in horror as I braced for the sound of her hip shattering. But almost immediately she was on all fours, scrabbling at me fast. Her face was ferocious and determined and she was making a beeline for my ankle, which for a deranged instant I thought she was actually planning to bite. But instead she swerved left, crawling into the bookcase. It was still lying on its side, so she wedged herself between two shelves, curling into a semi-fetal position. I tried to keep dragging it, but it was too heavy. 'Oh, I hope you're happy with yourself,' I hissed at her. 'I hope you're truly comfortable in there!' She didn't respond. I imagined her smiling, smugly hugging her knees, like some hippie chained to a tree. Invigorated with hatred, I hunkered down over the frame and tugged, exerting my entire body against her weight. The bookcase jerked backward, an inch across the floor. I kept at it. In this way, inch by inch, I managed to haul her down the hall. She held tight to the shelves, her knuckles bloodless. And even after the bookcase had come to a halt—safely back in my bedroom—she refused to crawl out.

I wouldn't allow her to win this way—not by attrition, not just by sitting in there until I grew bored and quit. If she wouldn't come out on her own, I'd smoke her out. And so, pitilessly, I began rocking the bookcase, teetering it from side to side like a carnival ride. Whenever it listed floor-ward her frail arm shot out as a buttress, palming the ground to keep her from sliding free. I rocked it at more acute angles, so that she'd have to support more and more of her weight; then I stopped abruptly, letting the structure jolt. I heard her thud heavily against the backboard. She was too proud to scream. I began beating on the bookcase. For five straight minutes I drummed a tattoo with both hands, repeating 'Get out, get out' in rhythm with the beats. I kneed the side of the frame, knowing she'd feel the shudder all around her. I berated her. How long, I asked evilly, did she think she could stay in there, with her old woman's bladder? I could wait all night. I told her she was being childish. I told her she was acting like a child. For someone who had lectured me on maturity, I said, she sure was behaving like an infant. Is this how she'd raised her son? I asked. Crawling into bookcases until she got her way? Still too proud to respond, she remained silent. I goaded her: Is it? Is it? Is this how she'd raised her son? Finally she shrieked back at me. I can't replicate the shriek. It was prolonged and high-pitched and hateful. But what she screamed was: 'MY SON IS *DEAD*!'

This actually did chasten me, somewhat. I grew quiet. She was not, or not only, the antagonist of my personal story. She had a past of her own, pockmarked with loss; she was a human being. Yet as quickly as this empathy rose in me, I stifled it—I swallowed it back like bile. Now would be the perfect time to try rocking the bookcase again, I realized. She would not be expecting it. So, gripping either end, I careened it left and right as forcefully as I could. While the memory of her dead son was still fogging her mind, I tried to heave her onto the floor.

It was then that Fredricka's hand darted into her nightgown pocket. I watched with dread as she fumbled—I felt sure of this—for a pistol. But what she withdrew instead was a cell phone. Still huddled inside the bookcase, she dialed a recognizable three-tone number. She just wanted me to know, she announced, she was calling the police. Excellent, I said, wonderful. What was she going to tell them? 'The truth. That you're abusing me.' So, I thought. She would portray me as the Violent

Criminal, with her as the superannuated Damsel. I heard only her end of the conversation, which she conducted in a screechy, beleaguered voice: 'Yes, *physically*... No, not hitting me... He's been rocking and dragging the bookcase... Yes, I'm *inside* the bookcase...' Et cetera. You can imagine how it sounded. When the officers arrived, I went downstairs to meet them. They were two guys, not much older than I was, and from the moment I began recounting the conflict—delivering, as it were, a first draft of my monologue—they asked the same kinds of sympathetic, incredulous questions that I have since come to expect: 'You brought it in off the street all by your*self*?'; 'She broke into your room and just *took* it from you?' I corkscrewed an index finger around my temple, signaling dementia, and they nodded in understanding. Poor college kid, senile landlady—what were you gonna do? The officers assured me that the bookcase was rightfully mine. The shorter one asked whether she was still inside it, like at this very moment, and when I nodded he bounded up the stairs with a boyish grin on his face, exclaiming, 'This I gotta see!'

You know how this ends. Here's the bookcase. The officers made Fredricka agree to relinquish it, and I took it with me when I moved. It's funny: at this point it doesn't even seem like 'lawful property' anymore—more like some big white trophy, a laurel the police awarded me. If you'll direct your attention now to the bookcase, between those middle shelves, you can see where she was huddled. Picture a crone cramped inside that space. Hugging her knees, glaring out at us. I'd do it all over again, if I had to.

4.

Ira Glass arrived at the apartment that Saturday. The interview took place in the living room, with Michelle and me on the sofa, and Ira on the ottoman opposite. Across the coffee table he aimed a silver baton-sized recording device at us: a shotgun microphone. Its sides were grooved with slots, and near the battery pack at the base was a blinking green light.

'So we're rolling,' he said, smiling bashfully. He seemed apologetic for the presence of the microphone in some way, as if it were intruding on a conversation between friends. He wasn't wearing the suit I'd associated him with—from Showtime's short-lived television version of *This American Life*—but was still dressed professionally, in a white button-down and charcoal slacks; and he leaned forward in a relaxed posture, elbows on knees, training a frank gaze on me through his trademark black-frame glasses. His salt-and-pepper hair belied his boyishness. He encouraged me to speak freely: any infelicities or flubs would be edited out in post. The green light blinked.

'Carleen told me about the bookcase,' he said. 'It sounds like a wild story.'

Behind him the bookcase stood empty. I'd removed all its contents earlier that morning, so that he could get a sense of its dimensions. But now he sat with his back to it, the desolate white shelves framing his shoulders.

'You have to hear him tell it,' Michelle said, nodding to me. 'I've heard it so often I could almost tell it myself. But his is the definitive version.' Ira smiled at her with a slightly quizzical expression. She continued: 'I'm just here as the prompter. In case he forgets anything. Under the floorboards, murmuring his lines.'

That seemed to be my cue. 'It was for my first apartment,' I began.

Ira relied initially on light questioning to guide me: how old was I, where was I working at the time. Soon, though, he lapsed into silence, simply letting me recite my story. I told him about the flat, and about my first chilly interview with Fredricka. I told him about finding the bookcase, and about her passive-aggressive Post-its. For the most part Michelle sat quietly by and

nodded. But when I got to the note about the 'undies,' she interrupted suddenly, patting my thigh.

'Tell him about the cats!' she said.

Ira turned to her and made a piratical, throat-slicing gesture
with his index finger, indicating the microphone below. She was
impenitent; he'd already explained that interruptions could be
deleted. 'Do the cats,' she whispered.

Ira pivoted back to me and said, in his soft voice, 'So what's
this about the cats?'

In truth, I'd forgotten about the cats. Over the years I had
gradually edited this incident out of the story's rising action,
and it must have been edited out of my memory as well. It was
just another tiff with Fredricka, superfluous, because it never
seemed as funny or absurd to a listener as it did to me. Not long
after I'd scandalized Fredricka with my undies, I found a typed
message on the bathroom door: a notice that the shower would
be mostly 'out of service' for the week. It seems Fredricka had
volunteered to look after some kittens from a neighbor's litter, a
half-dozen or so sick ones that needed to be quarantined from
the rest. Until they perished from their rare and contagious
feline blood disease, Fredricka would be housing them in the
shower. From eight to nine, the note promised, both morning
and night, Fredricka would remove the kittens, giving us all an
hour to bathe.

The point of that anecdote, when I'd originally included it,
was that Fredricka was a ludicrous hypocrite. She takes me to
task for hanging my swimsuit to dry: *that* is thoughtless; *that* is
an imposition. Then, not a week later, she dumps a heap of
diseased kittens into the shower, letting them writhe on the porcelain in a dying pile, pissing and shitting all over themselves.
The little pellets of their pestilential feces collected in the drain,
clogging its silver colander; rather than cleaning it in advance of
the posted hours, Fredricka simply swept the feces to one corner of the shower floor, creating a mound of waste. She would

clear the kittens out, but I would still have to tiptoe around this disgusting dunghill while I bathed, its runoff muddying the suds at my feet. Whenever relating this anecdote, I'd let my voice grow loud with outrage here, hammering home how absurd the situation was.

With Ira, however, I didn't get a chance to make this point. The moment I mentioned Fredricka's note on the door, he interjected: 'Well, that was nice of her.' He meant, taking in dying kittens. Caring for animals. He thought that this was her nicer side and that that was the whole point of the anecdote: that it was a counter-characterization, a humanizing exemplum, meant to deepen Fredricka or complicate my caricature of her. And since I didn't contradict him—I cut the episode short at the door note—that is in effect what it became.

Five minutes later, when I got to Fredricka's next Post-it— the one offering dishwashing lessons—Michelle patted my thigh again. 'Tell him about the note on the refrigerator.' Her voice was casual, but I could tell that she was driving at something. Ira glanced between us inquisitively.

'Which note?' I asked.

'You know. The one… "I'm sorry if I've seemed—"'

It had been years since I had thought of this note. As with the kitten incident, I had eliminated it from the monologue for reasons that were themselves now difficult to remember. I even found Michelle's freakish recall of the original version unnerving, under the circumstances. What happened was that, about a week before I decided to move, Fredricka left a Post-it on the refrigerator door, apologizing for her recent behavior. That was all. She never discussed it with us or posted a follow-up clarification. If she seemed grouchy or crotchety, the note read, she was sorry—she was experiencing a tough time and had to work through something.

Ira stopped me. 'Wait wait wait. What does that mean? "Work *through* something"? What, was she dying?'

I didn't know what it meant, and I told him so. I did know that I didn't like the tone in his voice one bit: that affected softness, its spittly lilt. Michelle had correctly identified it as Ira's sympathy voice, and I worried that the story was getting away from me. If I wasn't careful, Fredricka would emerge as too human a character—the kitten caretaker, the cancer victim—and I would look all the more monstrous for rocking the bookcase. Glossing over Ira's questions altogether, I skipped straight to the broken-plate scene. Her worst moment, for my money.

I'd recounted the bookcase debate, the tug-of-war, and her fall to the floor when Ira interrupted again. 'Let me get this straight,' he said. 'You're telling me she crawled *inside* the bookcase?' His voice cracked with mock shock. He affected an incredulous smirk and leaned over the coffee table, pointing the microphone at me. Carleen, of course, would have already told him every detail. But to humor him, and for listeners' benefit, I said yes, as if he were hearing it for the first time—yes, she crawled inside. 'May I?' he asked. He stood from the ottoman and walked over to the empty bookcase, eyeballing it as he laid one hand on its top. Then he tilted the frame toward him and lowered it all the way to the floor, so that it was lying on its side. Finally—and this I was not prepared for—he got down on hand and knee himself, as if to inspect the crawlspace, and without a word he crawled inside. Hugging his knees to his chest, just as Fredricka had, he looked out at us. He'd taken the microphone in with him, and the way he held it up to his mouth gave him a strangely solemn, buried-alive aspect: like a mountain climber in an avalanched cave, recording his final testament. 'So,' he said, 'to all you listeners out there. I just want you to know that I'm sitting *inside* the bookcase. Right now. My whole body. I've crawled inside, just like poor Fredricka. And I've gotta tell you: you would have to *really* want this bookcase to do something like this. It's cramped. I feel silly. My—uh—head's pressing against the top here. No dignity *at all*. And just think about doing this at seventy, eighty years old.'

'And don't forget,' Michelle said, 'that he was *rocking* it.' She stood from beside me and joined Ira at the bookcase, grasping the frame. Fredricka had wanted it enough not only to crawl inside, she said, but to stay there at the risk of injury. Michelle rattled the bookcase, in demonstration. Then, looking at me, she said: 'Show him.' I didn't move. 'Come on. Show him how you rocked the bookcase.' I glanced to Ira, scrunched between the shelves. His knees jutted to either side of his face, and his eyes looked wide and frightened, uncomprehending. Is this what Michelle wanted me to see? To understand that the fear in this face is what I had inflicted on Fredricka? In Ira's terror-widened eyes, was I supposed to see myself as Fredricka saw me? My worst self reflected back.

Before I had a chance to react, Ira recomposed himself, angling the microphone toward me and proceeding with the interview. 'Then what happened?' he asked. Evidently he was planning to stay in the bookcase. I would have to address the story to his hunched form. This seemed to be what he wanted— like a director he was drawing a lively, naturalistic performance out of me. Recognizing my hesitation, he smiled. So I strode over and glared down at him. I impersonated myself goading Fredricka: you're acting like a child, I recited at Ira—you're being childish. How much longer do you think your bladder will even hold? Is this how you raised your son? Ira smiled again and made waterwheel motions with his free hand, encouraging me to keep it coming. 'Is it?' I asked. 'Is it? Is this how you raised your son?' When I reached Fredricka's climactic shriek— 'MY SON IS *DEAD!*'—I actually did the shriek. In a scratch-throated witch's voice I lamented at the top of my lungs that 'my' son was dead, then started coughing uncontrollably. Ira and Michelle both laughed.

'Oh no!' Ira said. 'She actually *said* that? You must have felt awful.'

'Tell him,' Michelle added, 'tell what happened when you were moving.'

'When I was moving?'

'Her son,' she said.

My face flushed with shame. I looked to Michelle in appeal, but her own expression was blank and severe. In that moment I understood how thoroughly she'd prepared for this. 'Go on,' she insisted. 'Tell him.'

I had never told this part of the story to anyone else. In truth, it wasn't even 'part' of this story—not a coda or capstone—but its own narrative altogether. 'The Meanest Thing I've Ever Said To Anyone.' It just happened to involve Fredricka.

It was my final day in the apartment. I'd already moved the bookcase and was returning for the last of my boxes when Fredricka came into my room to discuss my safety deposit. There would have to be deductions, she informed me. With undisguised glee she began to itemize the different messes I had left: I hadn't washed one of the pillowcases—she would charge me for that; there was the broken plate—she would charge me for that; I'd left a crumpled Post-it in the wastebasket—she would charge me for that. And so on. I played along: 'What exactly am I paying for?' I asked. 'The labor of emptying the trash?' Oh, she cooed, I'd find out soon enough—I'd see what she charged for her services. Finally, in her obvious coup de grâce, she casually mentioned that I would also be paying for 'that bookcase that you stole.' I laughed outright. So this had nothing to do with the lease or the deposit: it was simply her way of getting the last word in. 'The police declared it mine,' I reminded her. She was ready for this: 'They had no right! It wasn't their jurisdiction!' I asked how much she proposed to charge for it, a piece of trash left on the street. Seventy dollars, she said—half what her neighbor claimed to have paid. This was so idiotic that I became incandescent with rage. Yet I said nothing, for I knew that the price was arbitrary. There was no point disputing it. This was the last word—at least where the bookcase was concerned—and I let Fredricka have it. But as I was walking out of the flat, I turned a final time to look at her. She was standing in the hall, watching me go, her arms crossed. Her dumb face sagged, as if in sadness. I felt it as a pressure building inside me. Before slamming the door, I shouted back to her—shrieked, actually—'*I HOPE YOUR SON ROTS IN HELL!*'

Every year or so, while lying in bed, I remember this sentence—I picture Fredricka in the hall, stung by my pointless cruelty—and I wince.

The night I told Michelle this story, early on in our relationship, I warned her that she would think less of me for hearing it. I even made her promise never to tell any of our friends. So when in our living room that afternoon she encouraged me once again to tell Ira, I looked at her in confusion. I couldn't believe she was bringing this up now, for me to broadcast on national radio. Except of course she was bringing it up. She'd likely come to the interview with nothing else in mind: simply to ensure that the story was told from all sides, that both Fredricka and I were characterized as fully, as comprehensively, as possible. If this meant disclosing the evilest thing I ever said to her, or indeed to anyone, then so be it. And if I wasn't willing to tell Ira—if I feigned forgetfulness—Michelle would be happy to tell him herself.

As if reading my thoughts, she nodded grimly. It didn't occur to me then that Michelle might have been staging this confession—with Ira in that bookcase like a shriver in his booth—for my own sake. That she believed it would clear my conscience to express remorse; or else make me seem—to Ira and to listeners—like the mature, compassionate, sensitive man she knew I had it in me to be. This did not occur to me. All I was thinking, at that moment, was that she was out to humiliate me. She wouldn't quit until the bookcase story was unsalvageable, I thought. And it wouldn't be enough for me to just admit my guilt. No, then—on top of that—I'd have to charitably consider all of Fredricka's possible motives. Maybe she had her *reasons* for stiffing me seventy dollars, I would have to concede. Maybe she was broke. Maybe she was bulimic! I tried to picture Fredricka listening to *TAL* in a few weeks' time, hearing my voice again as I narrated all this. Hearing me shriek—again—'*I HOPE YOUR SON ROTS IN HELL!*' If she ever told the story herself, this was almost certainly the way it concluded: That time, after my son died. And a strange young man moved into his bedroom. And terrorized me. *This* was the story Michelle wanted me to tell. She expected me to broadcast Fredricka's version to the whole world, preserving it for posterity in a podcast. I gritted my teeth. The thought of just laying the story, *my* story, at her feet like that—I couldn't.

Yet Ira and Michelle were both watching me, waiting. I had to say something. And here's the thing: part of me would have been happy to confess, so long as it never left that room. Part of me really did want to be the man Michelle wanted me to be. I quickly weighed the likelihood of Ira's ever actually airing it. He was still cramped inside the bookcase, waggling the microphone, and I remembered that mine was the story he was here to hear today. Michelle had said as much herself, q.v. prong number three: I was supposed to be the sincere, relatable narrator. *TAL*'s listeners didn't *want* a callous bully for a protagonist. If I deviated too far from this script—if I divulged certain cruelties to Ira—he could be trusted to just edit them out in post. Any mean-spirited or unsympathetic or unflattering footage of me would be left on the cutting-room floor, along with the flubs. And to be entirely safe, I could always email him afterward, asking him to delete it.

I cleared my throat. Ira smiled encouragingly, aiming the microphone at me. The green light winked. The important thing to remember, I remember telling myself, is that I am not this story. This story isn't me. I can confess it to Ira, and no one else will ever hear it. I breathed. 'It was my last day in the apartment,' I began.

5.

Well, our program was produced today by Robyn Semien and myself, with Alex Blumberg, Ben Calhoun, Jane Feltes, Sarah Koenig, Jonathan Menjivar, Lisa Pollak, Alissa Shipp, and Nancy Updike. Our senior producer is Julie Snyder. Production help from Eric Mennel. Music help from Jessica Hopper. Seth Lind is our production manager. Emily Condon is our office manager. Our website, where you can get our free weekly podcast: thisamericanlife.org. *This American Life* is distributed by *Public* Radio International. WBEZ management oversight for our show by *our boss*, Mr. Torey Malatia, who became *very angry* this morning, when I suggested we try a bring-your-child-to-work day. Nancy Updike just wanted to show her son the office, and here, here's what he said to her: '*I HOPE YOUR SON ROTS IN HELL!*' I'm Ira Glass. Back next week with more stories of *This American Life*.

Ekphrases

I.

THERE IS A FAMOUS PHOTOGRAPH TAKEN AT THE
edge of death: inside a car parked by the sidewalk are all manner of large dogs, looking directly into the camera. They stare
through the windows without smiling, with a peculiar severity,
like women and men in 19th-century portraits. The photograph
is black and white. Studying it, one commonly wonders, *How
did they get in there?* or remarks aloud, *This is something else altogether.* And indeed there is something unsettling about the sight of
those large animals, packed quietly into the abandoned car. The
photographer maintained that there were no dogs present when
he took the picture: his subject was an empty automobile. A
week after he developed the photograph, he developed cancer,
and within a year he died.

II.

There is a famous painting composed at the edge of death: a
broad cabinet is lined with cubbyholes, each of which is deeply
recessed and shadowed, and in each of which a dollmaker has
left a half-finished wooden hand; in the foreground, a small
boy stands beside a doll of a girl, both of their eye sockets
empty. Looking at the painting for the first time, one commonly
assumes that the hands are reaching out of the cubbyholes to
seize the boy and girl, who cannot see to defend themselves. On

repeat viewings, however, one begins to sense that the boy and the girl—eyeless, mute—are themselves summoning the hands, which reach not for either of them but for the viewer. The painting bears no signature. Its first owner killed herself, and its second owner killed his family before killing himself, in both cases within a year of having acquired the painting. Its present owner is storing it in a warehouse in New Jersey, where he will occasionally arrange a viewing. On the question of whether, in moonlight, the hinge of the girl doll's jaw unlocks, such that her mouth appears to open, he is casually dismissive: *That is a rumor.* Or: *I have never observed this phenomenon.* Or: *Her mouth, it is always closed.*

III.

There is a famous book written at the edge of death: it comprises descriptions of the face that the reader will see, looking back at them, if they look out the window to the lit-up window across the street. For every page a different face. The book was anonymously written and hand-printed, in a run of just a hundred copies. No facial description exceeds a paragraph, and while they differ in small details—the gender of the watcher, its age, whether the watcher's mouth will be open, or closed, or moving in rapid spasms—each description employs phrases like *horror-stricken face, dread face,* and so on. The book is the size of a telephone directory, with a plain white cover. It is said that for any given reader, the book contains one face whose gaze was meant for them particularly, at one particular moment in their life. Thus it may happen that a reader will sense, upon reading an entry, that yes, undoubtedly, this is the face that was meant for them—yet still never know when to expect to see it. Whether out their bedroom window, or a restaurant's plate-glass window, or out the window of an office building. Whether if they looked up now, or to the side now, or if they did not look. In this way every window comes to be haunted by the potentiality of a gaze. As for the many blank pages bound in the book, it is said that these are descriptions whose gazes have been met. When a reader sees the face that was meant for them, their entry in the book—the very ink on the page—is erased. As yet, no one has come forth to lay claim to a blank. To report what was written there, or what they saw.

IV.

There is a famous song recorded at the edge of death: a band performs in a nightclub, and midway through the performance the bandleader begins to address the audience. He speaks a few words in a foreign language, which are followed by a bandmember's solo; he speaks another few words, and another member performs a solo, and so on through all the instruments, the audience applauding after each performance. Listening to the song for the first time, one commonly assumes that the man is introducing each of the bandmembers by name and that they are performing by way of introduction. However, the more one listens, the more clearly one picks out the sounds that the man is making: they are words of no recognizable language, a dark gibberish, more like guttural noise than human speech. Each word is long, and clotted, and it becomes impossible to believe that he is introducing the bandmembers by name. Replaying the song and focusing just on the man's cadence, a listener might announce, *He is describing an apocalypse in a dead tongue*, or, *He is pronouncing an ancient curse*. And it is true that the wash of white noise at the end of the recording—that hiss of static, itself like a final solo—sounds so much like a tide bearing forth a curse.

V.

There is a famous film recorded at the edge of death: the camera frames the back of a chair, which is situated at the end of a semi-darkened room. Draped over the chair is a black shirt, which in the distance and the dark, as well as the graininess of the film stock, looks like the long black hair of a man, sitting in the chair with his back to the viewer. Indeed, for the first few moments viewers tend to mistake the shirt for a man's hair. *What is he doing?* they ask one another. *He's just sitting there.* The video, a static shot of this chair, lasts more than ten minutes: the shirt does not move, no one enters the frame, the camera is neither repositioned nor adjusted. When it becomes clear that the black length draped over the chair, perfectly still and quiet, is only a shirt, viewers assume for a while that a character, the shirt's owner, will soon be introduced to claim it. They wait for the moment when a human being will walk into frame and grab the shirt off the chair. *Why are we watching this shirt?* they ask. Or: *Is this all that is going to happen?* Of course nothing does happen. Except that in the last seconds, before the video cuts off, the room appears to lighten slightly. It even becomes possible, in this improved lighting, to see why the shirt had been mistaken for hair in the first place—for yes, it is textured somewhat like hair and tapers at the end like hair. Occasionally viewers laugh outright: *Just like the long black hair of a man!* or *If I didn't already know that that was a shirt...* Then, slowly, the long-haired man begins to turn in his chair, revealing a face that is like the nightmare of a face.

Two Guys Watching Cujo on Mute

'PEOPLE ARE ACTUALLY SCARED OF THIS MOVIE? I'll grant that that's a big dog. Sure. But it's not like he's bullet-proof. I don't get what's so horrific about this.'

'The horror has more to do with the like existential betrayal of the situation. The way a pet can turn on you. What can and can't be tamed.'

'Man's best… *friend*?'

'I mean it either scares you or it doesn't. Listen. I knew a kid once was afraid of dogs.'

'How old are we talking about?'

'Back in grade school. MacDougall Lewis. Spindly kid, pale, Prince Valiant bowl cut. He for one would hate this movie. And it had nothing to do with the size of the dog, either, I can tell you that. His fear. Couldn't even come to a sleepover without the dog locked up. And I'm talking your typical family dog: black lab, basset hound, Boston terrier. Even a little rat dog like that, the parents knew to keep it in back. "Is MacDougall coming?" That sort of thing.'

'What exactly was he afraid of? Did they ever bite him?'

'They never had time to bite him. MacDougall burst into tears at the very sight of them. Big blubbering tears. The kid just had a lifelong deathly fear of domesticated dogs.'

'"Domesticated."'

'I'm coming back to that. But note that that's what's so crucial about *Cujo*. What Dougall would hate and find horrific about the movie. Cujo's *not* just some wild hound—he's someone's pet. Look, he's about to get himself bitten. Nosing around in the rabbit's burrow like that.'

'The bat's rabid, obviously.'

'Yeah. Oof.'

'So Dougall thought the dogs were rabid?'

'No one knew what MacDougall thought. We just learned to keep the dogs locked up. Because if we didn't—say someone left the door open, oops, or the parents forgot MacDougall was coming over—there'd be that dreadful moment when we first entered the house. I remember once it actually was a Boston terrier. A little handbag of a dog. Mark Carlin's place. We were all coming in through the front door, and the terrier rushed from out back to greet us. Scrabbling across the floor our way. Yipping excitedly. MacDougall froze. Everyone saw it coming.'

'It jumps him.'

'Thing zeroes right in. Who knows what's going through his head, what it is he thinks he sees, when he sees it rushing at him: a werewolf, you'd guess, judging from the waterworks. And of course it leaps up on his thighs to try to lick his face, which just gets him weeping harder.'

'Christ.'

'The worst part about the weeping, of course, for MacDougall, was that it only confused the dog. And the little dog—sensing his distress and fear—tried you know to ingratiate itself and prove its friendliness by leaping up higher on his thighs and taking heartier, hungrier licks at his face. Completely humiliating. MacDougall begging us to get it off him, get it off him.'

'And? What do you do?'

'What *can* you do? Carlin there's calling the dog's name, but the dog just ignores him. Finally someone has to rush in and yank its collar, still shouting its name. This, by the way, was the very thing that horrified MacDougall above all, I was to find out later.'

'The name?'

'How it could ignore its own name. Anyway, that's more or less the way it would always play out. Before kids eventually learned to keep their dogs locked.'

'Yours too, I take it.'

'Didn't have a dog, growing up. But one time MacDougall did come over to spend the night, and my dad scarred him for life, inadvertently.'

'Hard to imagine you having a scary dad.'

'Yeah, well. He was a big guy. Burly. A construction worker, you know, a plumber. But built like a barbican and with these fat strong fingers that could unscrew screws and his sheer physical presence had impressed upon us all terribly, as children, my friends and me. MacDougall most of all. He was the kind of big that he got an ironical nickname: Cookie. "Mister Cookie," to MacDougall. We can watch something else, you know.'

'No, come on. It took us half an hour to settle on this. We go back to Netflix, we'll browse, bicker, it'll be another half hour before we've agreed on anything. This is fine. Just let it play.'

'All right, you're right.'

'So your dad and Dougall.'

'The thing about my dad was that he loved jokes and knew a lot of jokes and got a kick out of goofing my friends whenever they came over. But there was one joke in particular he loved to play. Practical joke. It starts out as just a story he's telling you, a memory he's remembering, this long and rambling anecdote concerning a road trip he supposedly took to New Orleans in his twenties. While there, he tells you, a group of his friends talked him into having his palm read by one of those Jackson Square chiromancers, a wizened old woman decked out in geodic jewelry and a flowing gown and a purple turban and heavy eyeliner, who my dad says he's immediately skeptical of but decides to humor anyway, for his friends.'

'This is a real memory?'

'Hold on. So he says that he sat on a folding chair at this woman's picnic table and paid her and let her take his hand in hers—and here, while telling the story, he likes to take your hand in his, and begin idly tracing your palm with one of his big fingers, a hypnotic massage such as he is supposedly receiving in the diegesis of the joke—but when the woman took his hand, he says, she squinted down at his palm and gasped, telling him that his was a soul rich in reincarnations. That his past lives were many and vivid and preserved with uncommon clarity in his lines. The whole spiel. He says he was expecting her to flatter his pride, tell him he'd been a Napoleon or an Alexander. And, indeed, when she started to trace a curve—and his own finger is imitating hers by circling your palm like—she told him that this was a mark made on his soul in ancient Rome. He perked up here, he says: Was he a Caesar? No, she told him—he'd worked with a crew on the aqueducts. Now my dad looks you in the eye and shakes his head and sighs: a *plumber*. Quips that he just can't win. You know, he was a plumber even in his past lives, his soul will be sweating and toiling for all eternity.'

'"No respect."'

'Right. Exactly. Then he says that the woman began tracing in another direction—he's still holding your palm this whole time, remember—and that she told him here was a second mark, etched into him in ancient China, where he had worked under similar conditions on the Great Wall. Which my dad obviously milks, mugging at you and slapping his thigh with his free hand, like, "*Damn!*"'

'I'm confused. Are you supposed to know this is a joke?'

'No, he's telling it like an actual story, like what actually happened to him.'

'So he goes on with the story.'

'Right. True story. The woman started to trace a final line in his hand, he tells you, this one leading down to his wrist—his own finger meanwhile tracing down to your wrist—and she gasped even louder this time. Said she'd never encountered such an eloquent line. In *this* past life, she told him, he says, he'd been a guard dog, a ferocious cur kept right there in New Orleans, standing watch on some levee job site for the Corps of Engineers. He was tied to a sturdy live oak by a choke chain around his throat and left out all night to bark, scaring off burglars or vandals.'

'A levee, huh.'

'Yeah.'

'"No respect. Even as a *dog* I'm a plumber."'

'Basically verbatim.'

'Is that the punchline?'

'Not quite there yet. It turns out he was such a ferocious and terrible guard dog, the palm reader told him, he says—and here he's like subtly and maybe even subconsciously *squeezing* your hand—that he would pass each night leaping against the choke chain to bark at passersby, yanking the chain again and again to its full length and gnashing his teeth at the darkness.'

'A regular ol' Cujo, your dad.'

'It gets worse. Because while burglars knew better than to ever jump the fence, one night a neighborhood kid wandered into the levee site by accident, and the dog—doing what it thought was its duty—actually snapped the chain to chase him down and ripped the kid's throat to ribbons. The next morning, the palm reader told him, the foreman arrived at the levee site to find the dog loose, wagging his tail and grinning, his muzzle and whiskers still sticky with gore. And when he looked past the dog and saw the boy's body, he was so outraged—like with guilt and revulsion—that he strung the dog up then and there, hanging him by his own choke chain from one of the oak's branches, so that that collar became the noose and the necklace that he wore to hell. My dad says he smirked and asked the woman how she could tell so much from one measly line in his palm, and she smiled too, and replied that it wasn't his *palm* she'd been looking at—it was the collar of lines around his throat.'

'Spooky.'

'And he tells you that she leaned forward to touch two fingers to his neck—now he's actually palpating his own thick neck, with his free hand, while still holding on tight and squeezing you with his other hand—and she said it was just as she suspected. That his throat's deeply rutted lines were a leftover soul impression, engrained in him from this past life's hanging from the choke chain. And she claimed that she could even feel where the collar had left a ring of scar tissue embedded under the muscle, mystically unhealed and metempsychotically preserved across his various intervening reincarnations. Here, while telling the story, my dad will stop palpating his throat a moment and chuckle. It's funny, he'll muse, but he really can feel the so-called scar tissue, right where she said it was. Probably it was just stress knots in the muscle, from work, and as for the cock-and-bull about his canine life, that was obviously an act: there had been no shortage of notorious news stories about guard dogs killing kids, and this was doubtless something she'd scripted to deliver to all her customers.'

'"And yet..."'

'Right: and yet, nevertheless, he says, it was impressive about the neck. At this point he invites you to go ahead and feel, right here, and he thrusts out his throat to you and takes your hand in his and gently guides it to his jugular, letting you run your fingertips over the leathery flesh there, kneading deep to try to feel the stuff yourself, leaning in closer and closer until—'

'I think I see where this is going.'

'Until without warning, when you're least expecting it, my dad springs forward like a mastiff from his kennel, eyes gone white and his mouth roaring RAR RAR RAR with rabid passion, the spittle flying in your face, gnashing his teeth at you point-blank.'

'Tell me he didn't do this to Dougall.'

'Well that's the thing. This was my dad's favorite joke. Pounced on any opportunity. If someone made an unwitting reference to reincarnation, palmistry, voodoo, or even New Orleans, he'd sidle into the conversation sly as anything and announce, you know, has *he* got a story about reincarnation, palmistry, voodoo, or New Orleans. My whole life, growing up—at all my parents' football parties, when the adults were gathered around the coffee table eating chips and dip and drinking beer and laughing—I would keep one eye on my dad. Because no matter what conversation he and the other adults were having, I could tell—I could just tell—that the bastard was sitting there biding his time. Lying in wait and listening for the least mention of reincarnation, palmistry, voodoo, or New Orleans. Assuming he wasn't insidiously steering the conversation in that direction himself. It could be like watching a cat hunt birds, at times—his grace and patience. It got to where you started to wince whenever you heard a newcomer say, some uninitiated friend, "I've been reading about reincarnation lately." You just knew it was coming. My dad didn't miss it. He'd been waiting for it the whole night. The gleam in his eye.'

'So, what? MacDougall comes over one weekend and says, "Mister Cookie, Mister Cookie, do you believe in reincarnation?"'

'Close enough. My dad and MacDougall are talking, and MacDougall says something that leaves him wide open, and I see the gleam. And from behind MacDougall I'm shaking my head like Noooo! in slow-motion, the way you do when someone strikes a match near a gas leak. But how's Dad supposed to know? We don't have a dog. He's never seen MacDougall burst into tears. And it's not as if I've given him any prior warning.'

'You let it happen.'

'I was transfixed.'

'You did nothing.'

'The second my dad took MacDougall's hand in his hand, it was over for me: I could only stand there, helpless and paralyzed, and watch with nightmare dread as the joke unfolded.'

'MacDougall falls for it.'

'Because of course he does. He's twelve, thirteen.'

'He leans in to feel the neck.'

'My dad hasn't barked for half a second before he's blubbering, "Mister Cookie, Mister Cookie!"'

'"Get him off me, get him off me."'

'Exactly. I don't need to tell you that my dad was mortified. He made it up to MacDougall, and we never talked about it.'

'Only MacDougall's secretly traumatized.'

'Never does come back to my house. Always an excuse, a scheduling conflict, so that whenever we hang out it has to be at his place. But his face darkens over at any mention of my dad, and I can tell he's getting real introspective and troubled. Stuck in a thought rut. Like the memory of my house—like my house itself—is something to avoid.'

'The shame of it.'

'The scene of some crime. Years later, we're in high school, I finally ask him—you know, "Doogie, what's the deal with dogs?"'

'He's still afraid of them?'

'I mean he's not bursting into tears anymore, no. He's got a little more grip on himself, and he's even more or less a normal kid, by this point. But if we're in the neighborhood, someone's walking their dog, he'll still freeze in this kind of barely disguised terror until the dog's gone. Trying to pass it off like he's checking the time or tying his shoes, but you watch his eyes, he's always got one eye on the dog. Not blinking. Pulse jackhammering in his throat. Which one day I finally ask him, like—what, were you bitten as a kid? Is there some root to all this? No, he says, nothing like that. Not that he can remember. And I say come on, there has to be something—you have to have suffered some traumatic childhood bite, right? Maybe even in infancy. Like a repressed snap or nip or snarl. Anything. No, no, he's quite sure. He even asked his parents, and they couldn't remember anything. It really was an irrational phobia, causeless, just something he was born with.'

'Bitten in a past life maybe.'

'Sure, maybe he was the kid my dad killed. But I say to him, basically, tell me what it is you're afraid of. Walk me through your worst case. Say we're in the neighborhood, a lady with a dog comes by, you freeze—what is passing through your head?'

'What does he say?'

'He says it's a fantasy. All his life, when he sees a dog, he can't help playing this one fantasy in his mind's eye. A kind of recurring daydream or waking nightmare. The fantasy is a big what-if scenario involving the dog. What if it spots him. What if it can tell he's afraid. So when MacDougall freezes stone cold on the sidewalk and stares at the dog from across the street, he says, what's passing through his head is that all these gears are turning: he's imagining *the worst that could happen*. He takes my example for an illustration. Say MacDougall sees a lady with a dog. An older woman, white tennis outfit and sun visor, walking a golden retriever on the opposite sidewalk. The retriever is trotting happily alongside its owner, tongue hanging out. But internally, MacDougall is already asking himself: *what if*? What if the retriever spots him? He imagines that it stops trotting and pauses on the sidewalk. In the fantasy, its body goes rigid with tension the second it sees MacDougall. The lady, oblivious, stops walking as well. Thinking the dog just needs to pee. And maybe it makes a show of nosing the monkey grass, as if it's interested in some scent there. But in truth it's merely buying time to eye MacDougall. Even as it snuffles the grass, it keeps raising its liquid eyes to peer clear across the street at him, meeting his own eyes with a prison-yard stare. What would I do if this actually happened, is what MacDougall's asking himself. And the answer is that he'd have to will himself to remain perfectly still. The last thing he wants to do, in the fantasy as in real life, is break into a run or any other sudden movement that will provoke the dog. Nor can he leave until the dog does, obviously. Whenever it lowers its snout to the grass, it keeps its wet dark eyes rolled upward slightly, to let him know it's watching.'

'You're right. He would *hate* this movie.'

'Too much grist for his mill—his fantasy's sinister enough as it is. Because no matter how long he stands there, the retriever just keeps sniffing the grass. As for the woman, she remains completely duped by this little ruse of its. She has no idea what telepathic transactions are passing between her dog and MacDougall. Maybe she bends down to murmur something into the creature's flappy ear, urging it to hurry up and "do its business." But MacDougall is its only business. It has no other business in mind. Something about MacDougall has set it off, he can tell. A mistake or misunderstanding has taken place inside the dog, and it thinks that he means some harm to the woman.'

'The woman being essential.'

'As in?'

'As in an intrinsic component of the horror of the fantasy. It's never with loose or wild dogs, the fantasy.'

'I ask him that. Claims to have zero fear of wild dogs. If he sees a loose dog in the street, no owner in sight, or even if there's a pack of them, his what-if scenario is over in seconds. Just reaches its logical conclusion. Oh, there's something I forgot to mention.'

'That "MacDougall Lewis" is an anagram for "Sic a dog: maul well"?'

'...'

'...'

'How long have you been working on that?'

'Pretty much all night.'

'It's that by this time in high school, MacDougall's started doing Tae Kwon Do: a blue-belt already, real little bad-ass in training. I mean he spends every afternoon after school in his backyard, punching posts for the numbness—got these knuckles like bamboo shoots—and doing flexibility stretches for his high kicks.'

'Great. Got it. Jean-Claude van Dougall.'

'Well the point is that, with wild dogs, the what-if scenario doesn't terrify him. Even if they attack him all at once, he figures he gets some bites, some blood loss, flesh wounds at worst. But he's sparred with multiple assailants down at the dojo. He knows that he can roundhouse kick the dogs or karate chop their spines or pry their jaws apart until they snap or snap their necks, if he has to, in the fantasy. It's an action movie for him. He loves it. Dogs are flying off him, he may as well have nunchuks. But with domesticated dogs it's different. That's how he explains it to me. He says that his fear is more emotional or even philosophical in nature than strictly speaking physical. He's afraid of being attacked not because of the injuries he might sustain, but because of all the emotional and even philosophical implications that that attack would entail.'

'So in the case of the retriever.'

'In the case of the retriever, it's integral that the owner remain oblivious. If she notices the dog's agitation at all, she has to misinterpret it, scanning the street for a squirrel or cat or something. Because another intrinsic component of the horror of the fantasy is how alone MacDougall and the dog are in their standoff. The owner can't have the slightest idea that this dog, her pet, has just turned on a primal or an atavistic dime, metamorphosing itself into a man-eater on its master's behalf. That's why she keeps such a flimsy grip on its leash.'

'Naturally.'

'Because the next what-if in the fantasy is obvious: what if the dog—maintaining spine-chilling eye contact with

MacDougall at this point—lunges forward in one sudden, terrible motion, tearing the leash outright from the old woman's
hand? That's what fills MacDougall with dread. What does he
do? All it seems he can do is remain standing stock-still on the
sidewalk, watching in terror as the dog—sprinting toward him
now and barking—churns the ground with its galloping legs.
There would be no point in running, MacDougall knows, for
the retriever would retrieve him in seconds. His flight would
only provoke the animal, frenzying it to a keener bloodlust. He
says he's conducted this fantasy countless times with countless
breeds of dogs—anytime one passes him in the street, his mind
automatically executes the thought experiment—and that of all
the different versions of the fantasy, for him the absolute worst
and most nightmarish version, the only time the fantasy ever left
him cold with sweat, was when he decided to go ahead and try
to flee. Says he's never even bothered budging a foot since then.
Doesn't even let himself consider it.'

'Clearly you wouldn't want to flee in a situation like this one
here: trapped in a station wagon, St. Bernard under the car.'

'Well what happened with Dougall was that he was walking
his bike home from school one day and he saw a greyhound
about a block off. A lean, ash-colored animal, being led on an
extendable leash by a jogger. The dog didn't notice him, but the
mere sight of it was enough to set off the gears of his fantasy.
So MacDougall paused there on the sidewalk while his mind did
its thing, working its way methodically through all the familiar
steps. He imagined the greyhound spotting him, stopping short.
There was the nosing around in the monkey grass and the periodic sidelong glances at MacDougall. The ratcheting tension.
Then at last the lunge that breaks the leash, the bark like clock-
work. Except now what was different?'

'The bike.'

'Right. This time MacDougall had his bike with him, in the
fantasy as in real life. And so he wondered: what if I got on

this bike? What would happen if I just mounted it and pedaled away? The answer, of course, is that the greyhound chased him. Even as he was looking straight ahead, zooming away on his bike in the fantasy, MacDougall could somehow still tell—as in a dream—that the dog was racing right behind him. He could *feel* it sprinting on its skeletal legs, keeping perfect pace with the bike. He could even hear the greyhound's horrible huffing, a choked salivary sound as its whole body heaved to keep up with his machine.'

'This is miserable.'

'And remember that back in real life MacDougall was standing frozen on the sidewalk, fantasizing all this. Meanwhile, in the fantasy itself, he was biking away, hightailing it down the middle of the road, which, like a road in a nightmare, was completely empty except for him and his pursuer. So MacDougall knuckled down in the fantasy, leaning into the bike's handlebars and pedaling harder, waiting for the greyhound to give up the chase.'

'Why didn't he just bike home? In the fantasy?'

'Then what? He'd still have to get off the bike to get inside, and the greyhound would be right there, at his front door. No, all he could do was keep biking and hope that it quit. Note too that stopping the fantasy is not a real option, for him: he can't simply open his eyes and wake up. The way MacDougall's mind works, he's in a kind of trance, an almost obsessive-compulsive trance. Has to answer every branch of the what-if for himself. Every decision entails a consequence, so he's stuck standing there until he's ramified the scenario to its likeliest conclusion.'

'He's made his bed, mentally, so to speak.'

'Pretty much. And in this particular case, he had cast his lot with biking off. So what if? What would happen? What he decided to do was keep pedaling, zooming blocks and blocks beyond his neighborhood, miles, with the greyhound chasing the whole way. He tells me that the fantasy became explicitly surreal and dreamlike, at this point. In no time at all he had biked outside of city limits altogether. He entered some deserted Hitchcockian countryside, pedaling down a narrow dirt road in the middle of vast cornfields, all while the indefatigable greyhound—which he still couldn't see but could hear the horrible huffing of—heaved its body behind him. And here a terrible realization struck MacDougall, he tells me. For at last he understood: the greyhound was never going to give up the chase. It had been *bred* to keep up the chase. Any other dog, any other breed, and he might have been fine. But all MacDougall had accomplished by mounting the bike was transforming himself into a racetrack rabbit, a robotic bait zooming away on a tantalizing circuit, which the greyhound was happy to chase for dozens and dozens of miles, at top speed, if it had to. Because this and nothing else was what it—the dog, down to its very DNA—had been bred for centuries if not millennia to do. MacDougall says that the logic of his dread was vertiginous. The fantasy was infinite now, he realized: it never *could* reach a conclusion. He would be stuck in his own head, being chased by the greyhound, forever. For the harder that he pedaled, the more determined the greyhound would be to catch him; and the more determined the greyhound was to catch him, the harder he would have to pedal. His terror of the dog spurred him to flee, which spurred the dog, which spurred his terror, ad infinitum, until MacDougall became mired in this morbid Möbius strip almost, self-perpetuating and impossible to stop. Even as his fear of being fed on fed into his flight, his flight was feeding into the dog's desire to feed on him, which fed right back into his fear, creating this like literal feedback loop of—'

'All right all right I get it.'

'He says that in the fantasy he kept biking farther and farther through the Hitchcockian cornfields until finally the fantasy self-aborted. When his mind couldn't compute the feedback loop, he suddenly snapped his eyes open: the street was empty. In real life, the guy and his greyhound were long gone. But MacDougall's heart was pounding and his palms were slicked with sweat, and he had to stand there another ten minutes before he'd calmed down. That was when he realized that fleeing the dilemma would always be worse than facing the dilemma.'

'The dilemma?'

'Okay, recall the thought experiment from earlier. The old lady in the white tennis outfit and sun visor with the golden retriever. The retriever is still sprinting toward him and MacDougall's still standing there standing his ground, because he knows—from his unspeakable experience with the greyhound—never to try running in the fantasy. So the dog is about to attack MacDougall while its owner watches, and the dilemma is that he has two options. One, he can spare the dog. Instead of killing this woman's pet before her very eyes, he can be manly and self-sacrificing: just shield himself as best he can and bravely let the retriever have at him until the woman calls it off. Figures the worst-case scenario is a bite wound or two. Maybe the woman *doesn't* call it off, and MacDougall has to wait for some bystander on the street to intervene.'

'Or option two.'

'Two is that he can defend himself. As with the feral-dog fantasy, he can dish out Tae Kwon Do with extreme prejudice, roundhousing the retriever or else grabbing its skull and twisting its neck. The only problem is that if he does this, then he's left standing there with a limp ragdoll in his hands, holding this dead dog, and when he looks up across the street, whom should he see but the little old lady in the tennis outfit and sun visor? Watching on in horror. The tears streaming down her grief-reddened face. Even worse in this respect would be if he *didn't* kill the dog, at least not cleanly. If instead it somehow managed to sink its teeth into his forearm, such that MacDougall had to kneel down over the beast on the sidewalk and pound its head into the ground with his fist, the way UFC dudes do on TV, trying to pry its jaws apart. And the whole time the little old lady watching on and weeping, calling out her dying dog's name while he brains it.'

'The name!'

'Exactly—this is what horrifies MacDougall above all. The fact that as this mankiller is trying to rip into his throat, some woman is calling, "Duke! Duuuuke!" Its name is Duke! It wants to tear him to pieces, and its name is Duke. Or its name *was* Duke—that's precisely what's so horrible. The little old lady thinks that this is still her dog, that she can call out "Duke" and that it will answer. But in reality Duke has left "Duke" far behind: it has already gone feral, retreated into some nameless part of itself. The woman can shout "Duke!" all day long and receive no response. It doesn't know Duke from Adam. MacDougall and the dog are alone now, stranded on the nameless side of its mind.'

'This being the philosophical dimension of his fear in the fantasy.'

'That there is something pre-symbolic inside the dog. Some primordial core. Like a little black tailbone, Tefloned against interpellation: the name rolls right off it. You can domesticate your dog, train it as a puppy and give it a name, but somewhere deep inside there will always be this wild residuum. The part of your dog that's not your dog. The past life—the species memory—that's still preserved inside it. Hence the horror of rabies: rabies is what uncages that namelessness.'

'Cujo stops being Cujo the moment the bat bites him.'

'This detail would not have escaped MacDougall's attention, no. He would invite us to consider the prominence of the dog's name in the movie. How people keep calling "Cujo!" How the movie's even called *Cujo*. The whole *point* is that the dog has a name. It's not a wild dog that's terrorizing people, it's somebody's pet. That's gone and betrayed its name. Which is a thousand times more frightening, from MacDougall's point of view. Now other monsters, they don't even need names. If it's a shark movie, the title's just the most salient body part: *jaws*—what's going to bite you. If it's subterranean sandworms, the title's just their calling card, their like signature seismological tocsin: *tremors*—what warns you they're coming. Naturally we refer to the shark as Jaws and the worms as Tremors, colloquially, but these aren't names the way Cujo's a name. What's terrifying about Cujo is precisely that *he's called Cujo*. Or that he used to be. Or so MacDougall would say, if he were sitting here with us tonight.'

'And so that's the philosophical component of his fear. Whereas the emotional component…'

'Oh sure. The emotional component is this very discrepancy. All the guilt he'd feel. That the woman, standing there and weeping over the retriever, thinks MacDougall is killing Duke. Good old Duke: Duke who licks her grandkids, Duke who chases after a soggy tennis ball in the dog park, Duke who can roll over and writhe like in a Western when you make a finger-and-thumb gun at him. She thinks poor Duke has attacked MacDougall, inexplicably, and that MacDougall is killing him. Whereas actually Duke stopped being Duke the moment he attacked. The state this retriever is in, he's not going to be fetching tennis balls or playing dead, to say the least. He's forgotten all that. So MacDougall is technically killing everything that *isn't* Duke: he's being attacked by *what's-not-Duke inside Duke*. And the heartbreaking part is that the woman can't know this, she just can't know. Watching and weeping like that, in the fantasy.'

'Presumably wild dogs dodge these philosophical and emotional complications by dint of—what?—they don't have owners or names?'

'There's no dilemma there.'

'But with a dog on a leash, every time MacDougall sees one, this is what's going through his head.'

'Well he's weighing it. What his mind is doing when it executes the thought experiment is deliberating. Could I fend off this dog awhile? Or is this a dog I would have to beat to death immediately? Is there a tree nearby I could climb? Or is this a dog that could outrun me to the tree?'

'Could I hide in the station wagon with my kid, like this mom here, or would Cujo just stalk around the car slobbering the windows?'

'And the owner, too. She's part of the fantasy's what-if algorithm as well. Is this owner a person who would understand? If I killed her dog, would she know why I had to do what I was doing? Or would I break her heart by doing it? In short, he's asking himself what the worst that could happen is. The thing you have to remember, it's the dilemma that frightens him. Its twin horns. More I mean than any physical danger posed by the dog itself. That's why a yapping Chihuahua freezes him up just as much as some foaming Doberman type.'

'Even as a kid, this fantasy.'

'His whole life! I couldn't believe it. But when I ask him about it in high school, he tells me that for as long as he can remember he's been conducting the fantasy. All those times in grade school, at all our sleepovers, *that* was what was scaring him. When the Boston terrier barreled at him and he burst into tears, and when he yelled out for someone to get it off him, get it off him, it wasn't being bitten that he was afraid of.'

'He was afraid—'

'He was afraid of what *he* might do to *it*! Afraid he might snap the little rat's neck, right in front of all of us. Even as its owner was standing there, yelling its useless, unavailing name.'

'And your *dad*.'

'Good call. MacDougall brings that up himself. He admits to me that he had been completely caught off guard by my dad's joke but that hands down the most terrifying part of it was when he had had to shout "Mister Cookie, Mister Cookie" to try to get my dad to stop. Because there was a second there when my dad didn't hear him. And didn't stop. And for the first time in his life MacDougall was brought face to face with what was nameless in *man*. He tells me that he had never conducted the fantasy with a human being before but that in that split second of fear he compressed the entire what-if scenario down to one instant, to one eidetic flash, and in the unfolding of the flash he saw that if my dad actually were to attack him—if my dad had some primordial core in him, which wouldn't respond to a name and couldn't be caged in a name, some past-life kernel left over in him from his canicular preexistence—MacDougall knew what he was prepared to do. He saw in the fantasy's flash, in all awfulness, what he was capable of.'

'Obviously not planning to wring your dad's neck. Twelve, thirteen years old.'

'No, but he admits to me—he *tells me this*—that out of the corner of his eye he noticed a steak knife nearby, lying on the dinner table. And in that moment, he says, he was worried he'd have to stab my dad. Right in the throat, where the dog scars were. The thought sickened him, but he knew he'd do it. He'd carried this murderous memory around with him for years afterward, he said. Too ashamed to share it.'

'Wherefore the face-darkening.'

'Right.'

'Jesus.'

'Oh you just know he's the kind of guy now, goes around poisoning neighbors' dogs. There isn't really even any question.'

'You keep up with him?'

'Lost touch in college. I looked for him on Facebook recently. I think he's working admin at the old alma mater.'

'What about your dad? You ever tell him about you and Dougall's talk?'

'No. No, I never did.'

'Hey now. Now *your* face is darkening.'

'I just remembered something, is all.'

'Come on, man. Don't hold out on me. Did Dougall poison your dad's dog or something?'

'No, nothing like that. I just never made the connection before now. Between this particular memory and MacDougall. I must have forgotten all about him by the time it happened. But talking about him tonight, it's funny. How I didn't see it.'

'Let's hear it.'

'The thing is, after my mom died, Dad actually did end up getting a dog. A little mixed-breed beagle. He lived alone with it awhile, over a decade, and around sixty he retired. He'd been doing construction for forty-something years, and the work had taken its toll on his body: overweight, bad back, heart attack. He was pretty run-down. Big guy—'

'"Barbican."'

'Obese. Had to stay sprawled out on the floor or the couch for his back half the day. Walking in Wal-Mart got him winded, so you'd see him in those little electric wheelchairs they have, puttering down the grocery aisles. Long story short he was not throwing Frisbees and sticks around in the backyard anymore for the beagle. But it kept him company, and besides, it was no spring chicken itself—probably a nonagenarian or something, in dog years. They fell apart together. The dog was in even sorrier shape, in the end. Stone blind for one thing, with these gaseous white eyeballs. Had to navigate the living room by memory, and was constantly being flabbergasted by the furniture. Staggering into sofas, nightstands, et cetera. Sometimes my dad'd find it trapped under a chair, penned in between the legs, walking back and forth and bumping off the railings. Just the most depressing thing. Incontinent, too. There was a while there it could still smell where outside was—the greenness of grass, sunshine—and it would hobble on its decrepit legs to the doggy door. Stagger out, do its business, stagger back in. But at some point the effort got to be too great and it just started going wherever: living room, bedroom, kitchen, it didn't care. My dad, with the weight and the back, he was in no shape to follow the dog around all day and watch for when it needed to go and pick it up and carry it outside himself. He took pity on it and let it have the run of the house. Nor were his efforts to sweep up its messes especially Herculean. Which after only say a weekend of neglect they'd need to be: to go find all the blind dog's crap and piss puddles around the house, and then to mop them, really was an Augean job, for someone in my dad's condition. So he lay on the carpet, stretching his spine, surrounded by all the droppings that the dog in its blindness had left, and he dreaded the day when it would finally die. For my part, I was ambivalent about the dog's death. On the one hand, it was my dad's only companion; on the other, I didn't exactly relish the thought of him lying around in a sea of its filth. Every now and then I'd ask him whether he'd considered the needle. Just putting it to sleep and giving it the dignified end.'

'What did he say?'

'Like it was his wife or something.'

'In sickness and in health.'

'"I can't give up on her!" "So she's an old dog!" "She wouldn't put *me* to sleep!"'

'Not like this mom here. Look at her. Beating on Cujo with a baseball bat. Cold-blooded.'

'If the beagle'd gone rabid my dad would have been absolutely defenseless, no question.'

'Old Cooge. Battered to death by his own neighbor.'

'I wouldn't count Cujo out just yet. He may look dead, but I bet he's got some gas left in the tank.'

'What was her name anyway? The beagle?'

'Clarabelle. As I said, I was ambivalent about her dying. I knew it was only a matter of time. Whenever I called my dad to check up, I braced myself to hear him say she'd passed. Preparing myself to console him and so on. Well finally I call one day, we've been talking an hour, and after a pregnant pause he says, "And there's some sad news about little Clarabelle."'

'Oh jeez.'

'Found her under his bed, died in her sleep. He's getting choked up as he tells me this. Eventually he just says, "And I think that's all I'm going to say about that."'

'Poor guy. Natural causes, though, right? This isn't where Dougall comes in?'

'No, listen. We're on the phone, and I ask him, you know, did he bury her? And there's this long silence at the other end of the line. And in that silence I recognize what a grotesque question this is. Of course he didn't bury her. How could he have buried her? My dad, can't walk ten feet in a Wal-Mart to pick up a loaf of bread, is supposed to go out in the backyard with a shovel and dig down in the dirt to bury his dead dog? But when he finally responds, what he says is, "Yep," in this quick, clipped voice. And I don't ask him any follow-up questions. Because I don't have to. In that moment I know: I know exactly what he did with Clarabelle. In my mind's eye I can *see* it. It unfolds in a vivid flash, the entire scene. I see my dad putting Clarabelle's body into a black trash bag. It breaks his heart, but what else is he going to do? I see him toting her down the driveway to the garbage can, wheezing the whole way—hobbling, from the pain in his back and from the weight of the bag—and slinging the corpse unceremoniously into the trash.'

'You don't think—'

'What else? He just couldn't bring himself to admit it to me. Too ashamed. Broken up over it. That he couldn't give his own dog a proper burial. A little stake in the ground with her name on it.'

'Her *name*.'

'In retrospect, in a weird way, it feels as if MacDougall won or something. Got his revenge. As if this was my dad's punishment for springing the joke on him, all those years ago. I can't explain it.'

'Karma.'

'Not that MacDougall could have even known about

Clarabelle. Or ever thought about me or my dad, for that matter—it'd been years. But I still can't shake the image of him rubbing his hands together somewhere, grinning at the news.'

'Working that MacDougall voodoo.'

'The ironic twist of fate. The cosmic comeuppance. Just as my dad had pretended to be a dog, and ignored the sound of his own name, so he had to lose his dog to namelessness. And not by way of rabies—not by a bite from a wild bat. But by *his own hand*. That's the tragic aspect. His punishment was that he had to throw her away himself, like some common greasy pizza box. He who had loved her so much and refused to euthanize her and treated her with human dignity was the very same one who, in the end, had to reduce her to this primordial core. Because by depriving her of a dignified burial, he was depriving her too of her name: she wasn't Clarabelle in that trash can, just some cold dead animal, which is what she would have to remain for all eternity, decomposing up on the landfill. And he was the one who had done it. He and no one else had cast her out, back into that dark part of herself, and for the rest of his life he'd have to live with that.'

'Almost like a mother burying her baby, before baptizing it, is what you're saying.'

'Something like that. Anyway, that's what was going through my head, when you asked me.'

'Heavy.'

'I mean I think Dad got over it pretty quick. He bought a basset hound about a year later. Hey—look at that. What'd I tell you?'

'Come on. You've seen this before. How'd you know Cujo'd come crashing through the window like that? One last attack.'

'I called it.'

'You've seen this before.'

'I called it.'

'Turn this shit off.'

'Yeah. Let's check if Netflix is streaming *Jaws*.'
'MacDougall afraid of sharks too?'
'Now have I got a story about sharks.'
'Oh yeah?'
'Yeah. Here. Here. Feel my neck.'
'Aw fuck you.'
'That's right.'
'Yeah.'

City of Wolfmen

<u>Directions</u>

THE CITY OF WOLFMEN IS THE CITY OF WOLFMEN only one night a month. For the rest of the month, it cannot be found on any map. Passing through a town of hirsute men, their forearms strong and calves thick, one may ask them where he can find the city of wolfmen: they will not know what he is talking about. If a gas-station attendant spreads a county map across the hood of the man's car and points at the highway there, his finger will fall on emptiness. The city of wolfmen is illustrated in invisible ink. The ink is visible only in full moonlight. The dot of it rises out of the map's paper one night every month, then withdraws, like a fever blister.

<u>Museums</u>

There are no museums in the city of wolfmen because no one remembers the city of wolfmen the morning after. Its citizens wake up naked in zoos and in parks, in beds of forest leaves and of jacaranda petals, in each other's front lawns and in the middles of streets, and the city is governed for one day by stupefaction. *Do you remember last night?* they ask each other, and none ever do. The tattered clothes and shed hair, unaccounted for, are destroyed, and cold creams are rubbed into the soreness of thighs. There is nothing left over for a museum, no artifacts and no history, because the city lacks a memory of itself. It is a zone of amnesia.

Transportation

All citizens lope in the city of wolfmen. If a man is on bicycle when he transforms, he discards it, and if a man is within his automobile, he abandons it. The only movement is the movement of paw over earth. For this reason the city appears congested with traffic jams, though these are only streets of empty vehicles. In navigating the main roads, packs of wolfmen will run over car and bus roofs as over a frozen river. Sometimes a wolfman, still in his automobile, will find it difficult to unbuckle himself, and on hearing the thud of his brothers overhead, he will whimper helplessly and claw at his seatbelt, unable to join them: this is the limit of sadness in the city of wolfmen.

Language

In the city of wolfmen all speech requires response. Howl from field is answered by howl from forest, which is answered by howl from lakebed, such that howl necessarily begets howl and dialogues are like great stretches of echoes. The law of communication is that to hear is to speak, and to speak is to pass the burden of speaking to whoever has heard you, as in a room of men who have been given the word *hello*. Some nights it even seems as though there are not multiple howls but only one howl, which passes from throat to throat, leaving one and burrowing in another, like a locust.

Dining

The morning after, a man will wake up with blood and its iron taste in his mouth. He will gargle with water until it is gone.

When he goes to pick up the newspaper, he will find a neighborhood dog, perhaps a golden retriever, laid out and gutted in his front yard. There will be nothing peaceful about the death: the dog's whiskers will not move in the morning breeze, neither will its hair, and this will unsettle the man; the only part of its body that will look asleep will be its feet, paws curled in at the ankle, except for one foot, crushed and bloody, which won't look asleep at all. He and the dog's owner will bury it. When the man becomes hungry later that day, he will be reminded of the dog—of the way that it leapt and yapped at streams of garden-hose water—without knowing why.

Buildings

What are buildings for in the city of wolfmen? It is an everted city. Outdoors—joy of unrestrained movement and howling—the wolfmen cannot conceive of an inside: their houses seem to them like boxes of silence, as though four walls were erected around nothing, around nowhere, to contain it. The sight of their own houses makes them restless. When the wolfmen see the city from its outskirts, glowing through distance and dark like ghostliness, nothing seems more improbable to them than that they should ever return to it. But then dawn tires and weakens them, and they gather on hilltops, panting, to admire the city's glistening buildings. Their same neighborhoods, built around nothing, around nowhere, seem finer now than forests or fields, and they trot home in exhausted packs. Under a sky pale as milk, thousands of wolfmen crouch outside front doors, whimpering to be let in.

Firearms

Few living wolfmen remember the village mobs that once hunted them. Only that the gunpowder of the rifle that fires the silver bullet is like grinds of nightmare, and the barrel smoke like a curl of nightmare, and the echoing report like the voice of nightmare, terrifying the very air.

Death

When a citizen dies in the city of wolfmen, his death bifurcates into two funerals. If a pack of wolfmen, prowling, finds a wolf's corpse prone in the forest one night, they will circle it twice before dispersing. And if a group of men, jogging the next morning, finds that same body—a man's now, nude and pale among the forest leaves—they will proceed to bury it. Even as a corpse the wolf metamorphoses: at dawn it reverts back to the man. Daylight depilates the body, shrinks its teeth. Coaxes the claws back into the hand. By the time the men find it, it is a man again and must be mourned anew. In this way the same death comes to inhabit two bodies. It moves, like a hermit crab, soft and white between its shells.

Love and Procreation

There are no women in the city of wolfmen. The population increases only in relation to the number of tourists who, passing through the city of wolfmen, suffer nonfatal attacks and stay on as citizens. Sometimes the men take lovers among themselves, though this is neither here nor there. Sometimes the wolves take lovers among themselves, meeting every full moon, though who can say whether a man transforms into the same wolf every month: perhaps the wolf is born at the first light of the moon, and grows old in ascendance with the moon, and dies at the moon's dissolution; perhaps a man has an inexhaustible number of wolves within himself and offers each month a new wolf; perhaps the love between two wolves is like the love of a man who falls in love in a dream, and if the wolves of the same two men should fall in love again the next month, then one might say that, as a coincidence, this is only like the dream that recurs, not that the two wolves remember one another, or the sweet smell of the other's urine, or beautiful feeling of jaws against the nape of the neck.

Ghosts

The city of wolfmen haunts itself, though it is not otherwise conventionally haunted. If a wolfman breaks into his own house one night and sees a photograph of his human shape on the mantel—smiling at a friend's wedding, wearing a tuxedo and no beard—he will growl at it, as at an intruder. Conversely, if a man detects the odor of wet fur lingering in his hallways, he will shiver, as at the presence of dead parents in dreams. In this way there are no haunted houses in the city of wolfmen, yet every house is haunted by something that the house remembers and the tenant forgets.

Astrology and Religion

Because the moon is the only influence and the only thing, the city of wolfmen considers the ocean its brother and considers itself an ocean of wolf. The wolfmen think of their city as a magnet that attracts moon: if a city of wolfmen were erected on the moon, the moon would close in on it, snapping shut like a rattrap. Or else they think of the moon as a magnet that attracts city of wolfmen: if the moon were placed closer to Earth, the city—its buildings and streets—would detach and float airily toward it. Beautiful moon: howling is a form of prayer; dilated pupils are a form of prayer. During eclipses, the men are like dreams of themselves, and nothing anyone says makes sense.

Destroy All Monsters

AROUND MIDNIGHT, UNABLE TO FALL ASLEEP, I abandon my bed to sit at my desk, an oak escritoire facing my apartment's western windows. Lying on the desktop is my copy of *Tom Jones*, which I was reading earlier this evening. Now I sit with it again, trying to pick up where I left off. But I find that although I am not tired enough to sleep, I am still too tired to read, so I put down the paperback and recrease a flimsy page corner to keep my place. (I have reached the seventh chapter of the fifth book, when Allworthy, Tom Jones's adoptive father, is convalescing on his sickbed. The last sentences I've underlined are those that Allworthy speaks to the friends gathered around him, whom he admonishes not to fear his death, for, he assures them, he has taken pains to spiritually prepare himself for it, unlike most men. '[I]ndeed,' he aphorizes, 'few men think of death till they are in its jaws. However gigantic and terrible an object this may appear when it approaches them, they are nevertheless incapable of seeing it at any distance'—'*Yes!*' I have written in the margin.) Giving up on *Tom Jones*, I stare out the two tall windows that overlook the backyard. But all that's visible in the blackened glass is the reflection of my own sleepless face. Or rather I should say that my face is visible *beyond* the blackened glass: the image of my face, though technically reflected on or in the glass, has an odd and ghostly depth to it, so that what my face really appears to be doing is hovering about three or four feet beyond, levitating outside my window in midair. My face floats hugely where the wide backyard should be. The reflection incorporates not only my image, but also the distance at which I sit from the window—a space the breadth of my desk. Yet while my face is all that's visible beyond the glass, I find that I actually can make out, if I peer closely enough, any number of visual details on or in the glass. The windowpane is dirty, for example, and I can distinguish all the particles of dust lit by the mellow glow of the desk lamp: little dots of gray constellating against the blackness behind them. Occasionally, too, insects will flutteringly alight on the pane, drawn to my room, no doubt, by the false moon of the lamp's bulb. Some of these insects I recognize, such as the large brown moth resting now on the glass, its two wings folded together like closed eyelids, balanced like a blink on its thin legs (I say that it is resting 'now' because, just a moment before, it was beating its wings in stationary flight beyond the window, not far from where my own face still floats, effortlessly). But most of the insects that alight on the window—aside from the moth, I mean—I don't recognize at all, couldn't identify if I tried; they remain entomologically ambiguous, just these little splinters with legs. And insect life is not the only life visible in the window. Crawling onto the pane, from the wooden frame to the right, is a neon-pink gecko, the back half of whose body still lies outside my line of sight. Pressed against the glass, its torso seems unusually magnified. For some reason the creature appears so close (though it is in fact four feet from where I sit) that its three-inch body looks hallucinatorily huge. The slowness with which it lifts each leg, the effort and heaviness of each step: I could be watching not a real-live gecko on my windowpane, but film footage of Godzilla on a television screen. Of course if I compare the gecko to another object for scale (my desk lamp, for example), I can tell that it's not much larger than my finger; but when I stare just at it, I'm able to magnify it to monstrous, macropsia size again. (At such moments I'm as fascinated by the sight of it as I first was by *Godzilla*, the

1998 American version of which I had to beg my father to bring me to see the summer it was released. Seated beside him in the theater, I remember peering up at the screen and waiting impatiently for Godzilla, whom I had only glimpsed in miniature—in tantalizing split-second flashes—in the television commercials. The movie's marketing campaign, I remember, emphasized the enigma of the lizard, refusing to reveal his body in advance. Instead city buses bore full-width ads reading 'HIS FOOT IS AS LONG AS THIS BUS,' and skyscrapers were draped with banners reading 'HE'S TWICE AS TALL AS THIS SIGN.' The actual design of the creature was kept carefully shrouded in industry mystery: until the film was released, Godzilla remained invisible. I was anxious to see him for the first time, so my father took me to the theater on opening night. Whenever that gigantic and terrible lizard finally did appear onscreen, I could not look away. I would enter—my father told me afterward—a trance of attentiveness, during which I was able to go whole minutes without blinking.) Now I watch as the gecko works to pull its hind section onto my windowpane. With its two forelegs, it drags itself gingerly along the glass, taking tentative, cat-burglar steps, peeling its toes from the window's surface. When the gecko raises and extends its right leg, it pivots its torso to the left, and when it raises and extends its left leg, it pivots its torso to the right, so that its body makes a sinuous, slow-motion swishing pattern as it swings its tail for balance (though I cannot yet see its tail, I can very well imagine its swishing, for the gecko's distinctive, saurian sashay seems to mirror those of its skeletally identical ancestors: the lizard, the dinosaur, and the crocodile. Indeed, the little gecko resembles nothing so much as a windup toy crocodile, or rather—considering the rubbery texture of the gecko's body—a gummi crocodile [for instance, the tricolor gelatin alligators that my father bought for me at the theater's concession counter before *Godzilla*: their tails red, bellies yellow, heads green. I preferred these gummi gators to gummi bears because, being much larger, they had a real thickness and density to them, which made them more difficult—and thus more rewarding—to chew. The slow, writhing slide of a half-masticated alligator down my throat made me feel, in the dark of the theater, less vulnerable: for I, too, could devour my prey whole, no differently than Godzilla. In essence, what I felt like was Death itself: an all-powerful and -annihilating predator, plucking each gelatin creature from its candy-box habitat and thrusting it into my maw. At the time I even pictured Death, not as a robed and scythe-brandishing skeleton, but as a giant, invisible lizard, one who would pluck children like me from *their* habitats and devour *them* in one bite. As I looked up at Godzilla, it occurred to me that this was what Death must resemble, assuming Death were visible. It was only when I glanced over to my father—his face merely amused by the lizard onscreen—that I realized Death might take a different shape for him. ((And how strange to think that, when I was a child, before I had ever read or indeed heard of *Tom Jones*—before I had even, for that matter, encountered death—my own conception of Death [[as a giant, invisible lizard, a presence that you cannot see]] was already consonant with Allworthy's))]). I see that the gecko has continued to crawl into my field of vision. About two-thirds of its body is on the window now, all four of its adhesive feet stuck to the pane. Where its toetips touch the glass the pressure makes them pale, so its feet seem to terminate in five little Tic Tacs of padded whiteness. If I lean in and squint at these pads, I can just begin to make out (or imagine that I can just begin to make out) their setae, the fernlike fronds of micrometric hair by which the gecko grips the glass, via so-called van der Waals forces. Afraid of startling it, I ease back in my chair and rest at my original distance. (Of course I have no idea whether it would even be possible for me to startle the gecko, since I can't tell whether it can see me. On the one hand, it's doubtful that it can *see* me, for its eyes aren't visible to me [the spade-shaped underside of its jaw is resting perfectly parallel to the glass, such that neither of the gecko's lateral eyeballs, welling out liquidly from either side of its skull, can be distinguished]; but, on the other hand, it might be able to detect me in its peripheral vision.) Even from four feet off, I can still make out almost every detail of the gecko's belly, the skin of which—a paler shade of pink than either its legs or back—is lilac, almost white in places, extending from groin to breast in a leotard of lighter-colored flesh. This skin of the stomach is so thin that through it I can see the dark forms of the gecko's internal organs, sacs of amorphous blackness that bulge against the lilac when it breathes. Its ribs make a tiny cage around them, like a canoe of glued-together toothpicks, and in its chest its heartbeat is visible, its pulse tent-poling the skin with quick, furtive fidgets (it looks like a fist beating off beneath a bedsheet). Meanwhile, as I've been watching, the gecko has finished crawling onto the windowpane, so now its tail is visible as well: as it tapers, the tail darkens, turning a merlot purple at its tip, and the whole thing lies plastered against the glass like a strand of wet hair. Having climbed onto the window- pane, the gecko seems content to pause there, as if catching its breath. Though just when I think that the gecko is at rest (just when I think that it might even be falling asleep, when I am cer- tain that it has nodded off and is dreaming on its feet [but do geckos dream?]), its head darts forward, taking a quick dig at the darkness. No other part of its body flinches (not even its tail), yet its head thrusts forward, like a snapping turtle's, and snaps, its jaws opening and shutting in a swift bite, as if feeding, al- though I can't see what—aside from the black air lying behind it in the night beyond the windowpane—it could possibly be feed- ing on, and yes, as its head darts, there it is, at last, its left eye, briefly visible and turned directly toward me, the lidless mem- brane turbid and pale, nor is there any question that the gecko saw me, for it was looking directly at me, unblinking, with its lid- less, milk-white eye. No sooner has it retracted its head from this first jab, however, than the gecko darts it in another direction, snapping its jaws at the darkness again, and then again in another direction, and again, stabbing its triangular, spade-shaped head here and there in the night. It almost looks as if the gecko is stabbing its spade head *into* the night, as if the gecko were trying, with the tip of its blade, to *dig into* the dense night air, dark as garden dirt, and so as if it were trying, with the troweling of its snout, to loosen the night's granules of packed blackness, to break the night up into clumps, as if digging a deep hole into the night. Again and again the gecko darts the blade of its spade head and retracts it, shoveling heap after heap of darkness, indefatigable as any gravedigger, as if what the gecko had to do—via the jabbing of its own head—was dig a grave in the night air. And this turns out to be not very far from the truth, as it so happens. For I see now that what the gecko is actually jabbing its spade-shaped head at are the little graynesses on my windowpane. Where the gecko's head darts, a dot of dirt disappears from the glass. So the gecko *is* feeding: it is feeding on the dirt of my windowpane. It is devouring the dirt, not of the night air, but of my windowpane, and so it is digging a grave not in the night air but in my windowpane, digging a grave with its face in my windowpane. (And is this what my own face could be said to be doing? For one thing, the reflection of my face, as I have already described, appears to be floating not in or on the windowpane but three or four feet beyond it. That is to say, my own face *deepens* the glass by four feet: its reflection constitutes a four-foot-deep hole in the glass; my face is *digging a hole* four feet deep into the glass. Now, a four-foot-deep hole is by no means necessarily a grave. But the only thing needed would be for me to back up my chair an additional two feet from the desk, and then the hole that my reflected face would be digging into the glass would be six feet under. In which case anything that I touched to my face—a hand against my cheek, for instance—would perforce be thrown down into that grave: the hand's image would tumble six feet deep into the windowpane, entombed in my face's re-flection. In this way, my face would be both the gravedigger and the grave at once, and it would be the coffin, too, for that matter, since it too would lie at the bottom of the reflection, at the very bottom of the six feet that it digs and that it is, deep in the win-dowpane where—being my reflection—its eyes would stare back at me. From the bottom of its plot, my face would seem to beseech me, unblinking and grim like a corpse's in its coffin. For all these and other reasons I come to believe that my face is dig-ging a grave in the windowpane, though admittedly in a different way than the gecko's spade-shaped head, which—unbeliev-ably—is still darting, feeding on the dust that speckles the dirty glass.) But no: the little graynesses on my windowpane aren't dirt or motes of dust, as I have all this time been imagining. For I see now that many of these particles are actually moving, inching their way to the left-hand side of the window. What the gecko is really feeding on are living organisms, bugs too small even to be identified as bugs—mites maybe, or monads. Well, I say that the little graynesses are too small to be identified as bugs, but what I mean is that they are too small to be identified *by the human eye,* or at least let us say by my eye, my naked eye, for the gecko's eye—its lidless, turbid eye—has certainly had no trouble identi-fying them, both as bugs and as sustenance, and in this respect the gecko's eye has, unblinking, missed nothing. As it darts its snout at them, the bugs flee and scatter, barely escaping its bite. Squinting, I can just begin to make out (or imagine that I can just begin to make out) how legs radiate from all sides of the gray dots, how the monads unfold around themselves these ciliated fringes of hair, which (either by whipping like flagella, or undu-lating in that underwater way of swaying seaweed, or [in the case of one mite] rotating back and forth, clockwise then counter-clockwise, like the buffers at a carwash) propel their bodies in leftward panic across the windowpane, away from the gecko, away from the face that is digging their graves, and toward the reflection of my own face. The gecko lumbers after them, rearing its head from side to side and snapping, such that its body recovers its initial illusion of hugeness. Its body even appears monstrous. Watching all these motes explode outward, like a sneezing, and watching their ruthless pursuit by a reptile whose own body is incalculable orders of magnitude larger than all of theirs combined, I am momentarily able to see the gecko through the mites' eyes: to regard it as the gigantic and terrible lizard that, to them, it must appear. A great pity for the fleeing mites surges through me. And yet when I say that I am 'seeing the gecko through the mites' eyes,' I'm presupposing that the mites actually have eyes, or else (since surely they must have something that could be anatomically classified as 'eyes') that they have something that *I* would recognize as an eye. In short I am presupposing that the *mites* can see the gecko through something like *my* eyes: not through photoreceptive pinholes that would merely register its motion overhead, identifying that darkling light condition as a threat (and thus not even seeing the gecko as a 'gecko,' just as an indistinct blurring above); but instead through foveal eyes like mine, which would take in the sight of the gecko, the full welter of its visual detail (its neon-pink skin and spade-shaped face, its four legs, its tapering tail). And since the mites themselves are microscopically small, I am further presupposing that their eyes would appreciate the sublime size of the gecko. The mites' eyes (I am presupposing) would render all the details of its body monstrous. So: no longer an indistinct blur (from the mites' point-of-view), nor just a regularly sized gecko (from my own), this behemoth lumbering after them would appear (through the mixture of our visions) to be all thick and thundering tree-trunk legs, and the whiplash swishing of an infinite tail, and the death-dealing snap of a grave-digging snout, and, finally, the awful whiteness of that eye, hanging as full and as huge, in the darkness above them, as a moon. *This* is the image of the gecko that I see through the mites' eyes, and that makes me feel pity for the mites, when I presuppose that they are seeing it also. But I am presupposing more even than this, I realize. For I must additionally imagine that the mites' eyes are connected up to a more or less sentient brain, generating thoughts in its little mite mind, which mite mind might, it follows, be able to register the presence of this gecko, and not only that, but also experience fear, panic, and dread of death at the sight of it. Yet can I actually imagine—as I watch the dispersal of the little graynesses on my windowpane—that thinking is going on inside one or another of them? What's likeliest is that the mites aren't conscious at all (or at least not as complexly conscious as other creatures [not even as complexly conscious, for instance, as the gecko ((within whose shrewd, mucronate skull—behind whose lidless, milky eye—I can very well imagine all sorts of *thinking* going on [[or perhaps only one sort of thinking, cynegetic thinking, death's-head thinking, the strategies and calculations and constant readjustments in timing that are required if it is to succeed at hunting mites]]))]). And once I admit to myself that the mites probably aren't conscious, I can no longer conceive of their being 'aware' of the gecko in any sensate way. Certainly not via foveal eyes. But not via any other modality of perception either: not through little pinholes that could register its caliginous shadow overhead; nor even through little tympanic membranes that could hear its footsteps on the windowpane, or else detect the vibrations that each of those footsteps sends through the glass (in which scenario the mites' bodies would be engulfed by the thrum of the gecko's footfall, a seism similar to the iambic 'foreboding rumble' sound effect ['da-DOOM da-DOOM'] that movies reserve for the laborious approach of off-screen giants [throughout *Godzilla*, I remember, I could feel this Dolby Surround Sound borborygmus, as if the darkened theater were itself digesting us]). Because if the mites *were* aware of the gecko, I reflect, they certainly would have fled from it long before it started darting its head and snapping at them. No, it's obvious that their sensorium is too rudimentary to perceive the gecko, and that they didn't even realize it was on the windowpane with them until some of the other mites began disappearing. It was likely just these traces of their brethren's deaths that—in a kind of Stygian stigmergy—spurred each mite to flee. And even then, they were probably aware only that 'something' was causing the others to die, not the gecko specifically. What horror: what the mites experience themselves as fleeing from—namely, this face that is digging their graves—must *have* no face. The gecko must be an invisible or liminally perceptible threat, a blank cause whose *effects* they flee. (In which case it really would incarnate my childhood conception of Death, which of course I then personified as a giant, invisible lizard, which is exactly [horrifically enough ((it occurs to me now))] how the mites on the windowpane must be experiencing this gecko tonight. Lacking the sense organs necessary to detect it, they could not look it in the face if they wanted to. It is hidden inside Death's spectrum, to the other side of the threshold of perception. And because the mites do not know to flee this giant, invisible lizard until it is basically already too late, they are like the men whom Allworthy disdains in the seventh chapter of the fifth book of Henry Fielding's *Tom Jones*, those men, he says, who do not think of death till they are in its jaws, and so who are incapable of seeing it at any distance. It is no different with mites than with men, I find myself thinking: when you bracket all thought of death within your mind, a blind spot must form, bracketing the sight of Death before your eyes.) Sitting up straight at my desk, I watch as the mites flee this lizard that they cannot see. The little gray dots of them on my windowpane drift steadily toward the reflection of my face, like iron filings swarming a magnet. Their cilia propel them slowly, though, and it will be a few minutes yet before the nearest of them reaches my right cheek. For its part, the gecko seems to have given up the chase. Or perhaps it is only resting a moment to digest. It stands now in the middle of the pane, its four feet planted firmly against the glass. Its sides expand and deflate in a shallow breathing, and its heart, again frantic, is visible once more beneath the lilac of its skin. It has fed well. I fold my hands behind my head and lean back in my chair, putting an extra foot of perspective between the gecko and me. Looking at it like this, I find that I'm unable to keep seeing it through the mites' eyes. When it is not hunting the mites, the gecko (so far from resembling a Deathlike reptile) seems harmlessly small, stuck to my window like a stick-on star. Its stomach, chewy-looking and pale, is shrunk to gummi-gator size again. My attempts at magnifying it don't seem to be working anymore. Which is a shame, for I had been growing—almost despite myself—hypnotized by the horror unfolding on my windowpane. It was as if a miniature kaiju film had been arranged for my private viewing: as if the mites were men, flooding the streets of an imperiled city; and as if the gecko were Godzilla, a nuclear lizard twice as tall as a skyscraper. Except now that it is impossible to believe that the mites are conscious and panicking, or that they are even aware of the gecko at all, the gecko cannot be construed, from any creature's point of view, as monstrous. For me to feel any frisson at the gecko's feeding, I realize (for the gecko to continue to incarnate Death), I would need to go further than simply *anthropomorphizing* the mites, pretending that they're conscious like men. I would have to pretend that they *are* men, regarding each gray dot on my windowpane as a human life. Then, when I watched those dots fleeing the gecko, I might be able to experience some of the catharsis that I felt during *Godzilla*, when I could watch actual human beings fleeing an actual giant lizard. Now, as the gecko resumes its ruthless pursuit of the dots, I try to pretend that that is what I am watching: that Godzilla (the gecko) is pursuing humans (gray dots), all of whom only appear to be small (to be a gecko and gray dots) due to some virtual distance between us. It takes great imaginative discipline for me to sustain this illusion, and I find that, in my sympathies for the gray dots, I keep wavering, regarding them as men one moment and mites the next. What this instability and, indeed, double aspectuality of the dots (their toggling back and forth, I mean, between mites and men) reminds me of is that famous line from *King Lear,* which I was assigned to read in high school and haven't read since, though I remember both the line in question and the juvenile marginalia that I scrawled beside it. The line reads—in da-DOOMing iambs—'As flies to wanton boys are we to the gods,' and my marginalia consisted of scribbling a line first through the *the* and then through the *s* of *gods*; replacing the little *g* of *gods* with an uppercase *G*; and then writing (trailing after the modified *God*) 'zilla'; that is, I emended the line so that it read (with editorial markup) 'As flies to wanton boys are we to ~~the g~~Godszilla.' I don't know why I thought this was so amusing then (perhaps it was simply the collision of cultures, high [seventeenth-century English Renaissance theater] with low [Japanese *kaiju* films]; or perhaps it was that, even in high school, I had lingering associations between giant lizards and Death), but at that point in my intellectual development, the thought of a man in a Godzilla suit waddling out onto the Globe Theatre's stage and vaporizing Goneril with his atomic breath was enough to make me bark with laughter, right in the middle of my second-period English class. Now, of course, the image doesn't even make me smile; I have outgrown the joke. Nevertheless, I find its relevance to the spectacle on my windowpane (or rather the relevance, not of the image, but of the marginalia itself: 'As flies to wanton boys are we to Godzilla') fascinating. For, in their double aspectuality, the gray dots manage to occupy both positions of this emended simile simultaneously: when considered as they are in reality (mites), they are flies to wanton boys, and yet, when considered as they are in my imagination (humans), they are men to Godzilla. In the first of these aspects, I am the wanton boy, I suppose, and then the gecko—it goes without saying—is Godzilla. Though it must be said that the gecko does not in the least resemble Godzilla. Whereas the gecko crawls on all fours, Godzilla was traditionally bipedal; and whereas the gecko's smooth skin is neon pink, Godzilla's squamous skin was dark as charcoal; and whereas the gecko's back is bare (though I cannot see the gecko's back, I can very well imagine that it is bare), Godzilla's was lined with that stegosaural cordillera of spiky dorsal plates, which studded the length of his spine down to the tip of his tail, where the dense aggregate of jagged spicules (like clusters of rock crystal) could be swung into his enemies to devastating effect; and, finally, whereas the gecko's eye is turbid and pale, Godzilla's own eyes were vitreous and clear, narrowed beneath his haček-shaped unibrow (a distinct V formation of lighter-colored scales, which gave him a constantly angry and aggrieved appearance). With that said, it's still easier to pretend that the gecko is Godzilla than that the little gray dots are men. Refocusing on the windowpane, I watch the dots flee leftward toward my reflection, and as they run I can begin to imagine their fear, panic, dread of death. I am even able to summon surges of pity for them once more, visualizing the looks on their faces. What I'm technically visualizing is the looks on the faces of the Japanese actors in old Godzilla films, and one look and one face in particular: the look—which I seem to remember from these movies' crowd sequences, whenever a mob of people is stampeding down a street with their backs to the camera—is that of the inevitable 'Lot's Wife' (that is, the one man or woman who cannot forbear glancing back at what it is they are fleeing, and so who break off from the rest of the pack to pause briefly, turning their head over their shoulder toward the camera, just to steal a glimpse up at Godzilla, for which glimpse they pay a ghastly price indeed, not only because the sight is horrific [the expression on their face is always one of abject terror, the mouth hanging open in a mute howl and the eyes widened in shock ((though occasionally the howl is not mute at all, but shrill and diphthongal—a sustained 'Aieeeeeeeee!'—often accompanied by a pointing finger))] but also because even the second or two that it takes for them to glance at Godzilla is enough time for Godzilla to catch up with them, that is, to be bearing down on them at that very moment, such that this poor Lot's Wife has no time to do anything but stand there paralyzed, like a pillar of salt, looking their death in the face, as they wait for the shadow of Godzilla's taloned foot to race down and consume them [when the foot itself races down, unceremoniously squashing the actor beneath it, I seem to remember that the accompanying foley effect was a 'splat' or 'squish' noise. That is doubtless what the people in the fleeing crowd would hear, along with Godzilla's iambic da-DOOMing, and the sound of it would be like a whip at their backs: by the sound of each *squash*, they would know now not to turn around like Lot's Wife, not to steal even the least glimpse of the giant lizard that was pursuing them; and so, unseen, Godzilla would be—in effect and in a manner of speaking—a giant, *invisible* lizard, this Death whose victims cannot look at it, at least not until they are already in its jaws]). At any rate, that is the expression that I imagine on the faces of the dots on my windowpane, the Lot's Wife expression (the sight of which terrified me almost as much as Godzilla himself when I was a child, and which, for a while, I assumed *all* corpses bore on their faces [even years later I was unable ((last summer, at his funeral)) to look down into the coffin at my father's face]). Nor would the dots' Lot's Wife expressions be unjustified, for even as they close slowly in on my own cheek, Godzilla—lumbering in the general direction of my face as well—closes in less slowly on them. But no: they may not be headed toward my cheek at all. For I notice, for the first time in many minutes, that that brown moth—the moth that had, earlier tonight, fatigued itself in stationary flight in the air beyond my window—is still poised in the exact same place on the glass, far to the left-hand side, such that it is in *its* direction that the men are fleeing and that Godzilla is moving. Though, naturally, the men and Godzilla cannot be moving in the direction of just any regularly sized moth. If human beings and a giant lizard were coplanar with a tiny moth on my windowpane, it would throw everything out of scale, disrupting the reality of the film. Rather, what I must try to imagine—in order to maintain the illusion—is that the moth, no longer a small insect, is in fact the same size as Godzilla. My only option, it would seem, is to cast the insect in the role of Mothra, that monstrous and lepidopterous island deity who appeared in her own series of Toho Company Ltd.'s films (which tended to portray her not as a monster, but as a benevolent protector or guardian angel of her island worshipers, a Phoenix-like symbol of resurrection and rebirth), and who also showed up from time to time in the Godzilla movies, typically to engage the so-called King of Monsters in battle (most famously, and originally, in *Mothra vs. Godzilla*). Indeed, this bit of casting should work out perfectly. Because if any monster movie is being microscopically restaged on my windowpane tonight, it is without a doubt *Mothra vs. Godzilla*. Was not the plot of that movie that Godzilla, roused from the sea by typhoon waves, arrives to terrorize a beachside city, where mobs of Japanese civilians flee helplessly through the streets, and where the whiplash swishing of his infinite tail halves buildings at a blow (they collapse like scythed grass), and where the impotent Japanese air force sends squadron after squadron of sleek and expensive fighter jets to launch missile strikes against Godzilla (only to find that these same sleek and expensive fighter jets are, to Godzilla, 'as flies to wanton boys'), and where it really begins to look as if that implacable lizard is going to stomp each and every building into the ground, until at last one brave group of civilians (the protagonists, in fact) fly to a nearby island where Mothra lives and beg the island's animistic natives for a minute of Mothra's time, beg them, that is, for the privilege of paying court to their monstrous and lepidopterous deity, whom the visitors are finally allowed to supplicate, and who finally agrees (Mothra does) to flutter over to the mainland and defeat Godzilla, or, failing that, at least to retard his awful rampage? And is that not the very thing that the men on the surface of my windowpane appear to be doing? Their little crowd of gray dots has been moving steadily toward Mothra: they seem to be fleeing Godzilla for *her*, for the goddess or guardian angel that—to them—the brown moth must appear (a life force perfectly matched against the gecko's incredible death force). And once they do eventually reach her, their last resort, surely, will be to beg that insect to combat the giant lizard on their behalf. At this point I actually lean forward in my desk chair, as if in a theater seat, genuinely enthralled. It's as if all the elements on my windowpane—the mites, the moth, the gecko—are staging an adaptation of *this* monster movie specifically, a 1964 *kaiju* film that I haven't seen since I was twelve years old. And how faithful will it be, the adaptation, I wonder? I try to remember the film's ending, but memory fails me. I can't even remember who vanquished whom. All I can bring to mind are stray images from the climactic battle, fought in broad daylight, as I recall, on the sandy beach (I think) of the seaside city that Godzilla had been terrorizing. What I seem to remember is Mothra flying in place in the blue sky above Godzilla, hovering in the air beside him, and maintaining that stationary flight—just as my moth had—by beating her wings into a blur, such that the rapid blinking of these vast wings (not pale brown like my moth's wings, but the deep orange of late pumpkin or dehydrated urine, and decorated all over with black eyespots) was powerful enough to generate heavy wind, downward gusts of vortical and (in Mothra's case) gale-force wind, which not only sustained Mothra in her hovering, but actually knocked Godzilla over, after he could no longer go on stubbornly shouldering it and digging his talons into the sand. And I seem to remember how beleaguered and small Mothra looked as she struggled to hover in place, how as her great wings beat she was blown back by the recoil of the gusts she was unleashing and how she had to fight (curling her thorax into a comma of strain) just to stay put. As for Godzilla's counterattack, I have no trouble at all recalling the blue-white beam of his iconic atomic breath, a cheaply animated flame effect that was employed in every film, postproductively roto-scoped from out of the costume's open mouth, where it gushed forth in steady streams of flicker and glow, half-laser blast and half-bile, like some lightsaber of chyme that Godzilla was vomiting onto his enemies (he even sometimes doubled over, so that he could better direct the flow of his own atomic breath, spewing it across all the tanks at his feet), which energy beam you could always tell he was charging up whenever a cartoon blue aura began to outline his dorsal plates, and which was hot enough to melt the shells of the tanks. Whether or not it was hot enough to melt Mothra I am powerless to recall. I suspect that the reason I can't remember the outcome of that climactic battle is not only that I haven't seen the movie itself (or any Godzilla film) since I was twelve years old, but also that, when I was twelve years old, the totality of my exposure to Toho's Godzilla films consisted of a single sleepless evening: a Saturday that same summer, a week after I saw the American version, when a cable station was broadcasting a midnight marathon of the original Godzilla series (including *Mothra vs. Godzilla*, as well as the battle-royal entry *Destroy All Monsters*). Earlier in the week I had spotted the marathon's listing in the latest *TV Guide*, a copy of which always lay on my parents' coffee table. While I had never seen one of the Japanese Godzilla films before, I assumed he would be no less frightening (no less Deathlike a reptile) than his American counterpart. So when Saturday arrived I lay impatiently in bed until around midnight, after my parents had gone to sleep, and then crept out into the living room. The marathon's inaugural entry (*Godzilla*) was already underway: the image onscreen, in grainy black-and-white, was a close-up of Godzilla's face, the jaws of his snout—flat and sharp as a shovel—widened to emit his trademark roar. The sound of it was galvanizing (I lowered the volume so that it wouldn't wake my parents). In that first flush of excitement, I was ready to stay awake all night, for the full eight hours of the marathon. In reality, I started flagging after thirty minutes, my head nodding against my will. I don't remember when I fell asleep for good (at some point I was woken in the dark by my father, who turned off the TV and led me by hand back to bed), but I made it through at least two or three films in this half-conscious state, constantly jolting up and goggling my eyes. Eventually my mind must have become completely frayed with fatigue (the parentheses between dreams and waking turned permeable) because I could not blink even for a second without falling asleep. As soon as my eyelids lowered I began to dream, split-second dreams or micro-dreams, seamless continuations of whatever I had just been seeing. So if, with my eyes open, I saw on the television screen Godzilla lifting his leg to take a step, then the very moment that my eyelashes met I would see (or dream I saw) Godzilla lowering his foot to finish that step. And if, instead of jolting awake at this point, I simply kept on dreaming, then I would see Godzilla take another step, and another, leaving the television screen far behind him as he descended deeper into my mind. There, my unconscious would weave a dream around him, modeling it on the movie I had just been watching and so doing its best to construct a habitat amenable to the lizard, a kind of oneiric terrarium where Godzilla would not feel out of place. The settings of these dreams would be the same seaside cities that Godzilla had just, on the television screen, been terrorizing; and the characters of the dreams would be the same military personnel and scientists who, in the movie, had just been trying either to pulverize or to propitiate Godzilla; and Godzilla (oblivious that he had left behind his television habitat for my unconscious habitat: devoured live—so to speak—by my dreaming eye) would resume razing buildings and swatting at fighter jets without missing a beat. Given that these were the conditions under which I viewed that climactic battle between Mothra and Godzilla—hypnagogic and groggy—it's no wonder that I can no longer remember the outcome. Even if the mites, the moth, and the gecko were to stage a perfectly faithful windowpane adaptation tonight—even if they were to behave exactly as their cinematic correlatives did—I would have no way of knowing. Watching them now, I rub my eyes to refresh myself, as if trying once more to stay awake for this movie. Of course, all I am really watching are some unsuspecting microfauna, comporting themselves in a thoroughly banal, nocturnal way: the moth resting, the mites fleeing, the gecko stalking and feeding. If the plotline of *Mothra vs. Godzilla* can be projected onto these activities, it is only because I myself am doing it. It is an adaptation staged by *my* eye (my two dark eyes, staring back at me from my reflection in the glass), or, more accurately, by my mind's or my memory's eye, which, like the astronomer's eye, confronted with a night sky's patternless points of light, casts constellations over all the chaos that it sees. (I remember my father teaching me the constellations in our backyard: he encouraged me to visualize those mythological silhouettes as nets, interpretive meshworks that could be cast over stars to ensnare them in narratives. As if astronomy were just a long slow mythological trawl, pulling in the heavy glittering, each night, of its mythological haul.) And how strange to think that my twelve-year-old self—fighting to stay awake throughout the conclusion of *Mothra vs. Godzilla*; falling asleep and dreaming brief *Mothra vs. Godzilla* dreams—was in a way preparing for a night like this one: when the same unconscious mechanisms that generated those *Mothra vs. Godzilla* dreams would be able to project them not onto the mind's eye or an inner eyelid, but onto a second-story windowpane. For that is all that this window is: a kind of dream that I am having. The very moment that the gecko crawled onto the glass, I realize, it must have been entering its own oneiric terrarium. And presiding all the while over this terrarium—reflected in the windowpane, diffused throughout its surface, just as my identity would be dissolved through every inch of a dream—is my own face: huge, somber, and sleepless. Though the mites, the moth, and the gecko cannot see my face, it registers every movement of theirs in its transparent skin, which is as one with the glass that reflects it. Nothing steps that does not send a vibration through my face. Interestingly, however, none of the creatures have stepped yet *onto* my face. My reflection remains the leftmost element in the windowpane. Directly to my right, the moth is still perched in place, resting on its thin legs. Languorously it unfolds and refolds its brown wings, as if blinking. Directly to *its* right, a nebula of mites is just beginning to unfurl a tendril of gray dots toward its feet. And rightmost yet is the gecko. Pivoting its torso, the gecko unpeels the setae of the toetips of its left forefoot from the glass and lifts the leg up into the air. When it lowers its foot, I think, it will be as if it is stepping deeper into my dream. And the effect will become only more pronounced once the gecko, moving inexorably leftward, actually begins crawling over the reflection of my face. Then it will plant its setae onto my cheek, onto the bridge of my nose and onto my dark eyes; it will pivot its torso over the temples of my skull, suctioning and unsuctioning its feet; and as it crawls across my transparent forehead—its body showing through the reflection of my skin, visible within it like a star behind a cloud—it will be descending quite literally into my mind. Except why wait for it to reach me? I scoot my chair a few inches to the right, leaning my elbows onto the desk and positioning the reflection of my face on the patch of glass directly in between the gecko and the mites. Now if the gecko wants to reach its prey—or to confront their guardian the moth—it will have to cross my face. The gecko pauses. The foot that it has lifted is brought down again, precisely where it was. Its heart beats nervously against its skin. Its tail swishes from side to side. Did it somehow detect my reflection in the windowpane? Did it see my face rush toward it—this huge disembodied head, twenty times its size, gliding across the opposite side of the glass—and does it see it now, an obstacle between itself and the mites? No, it is impossible: my face, however gigantic and terrible an object, must be invisible to the gecko. And whatever it was that caused the gecko to stop short (perhaps the scraping of my chair against the wooden floor) must no longer be a consideration, for it lifts its leg again and steps forward. I lean back in my chair, putting another two feet between myself and the desk, such that the reflection of my face is not four, but, yes, *six feet deep* in the windowpane, and such that, even as the gecko approaches it, my face is *digging a grave in the windowpane*. Now, when the gecko finally does cross over, it will perforce be thrown down into that grave: its body will tumble six feet deep into the windowpane, entombed in my face's reflection. I turn my head in profile to the right, so that my reflection is made to face the gecko in the glass. (Sitting like this, I can no longer look my reflection in the face: unable to see it there—lying at the bottom of the six feet that it digs and that it is—I feel as though I am averting my gaze from a grave just as I did last summer.) I squint at the window out of the corner of my left eye, watching as the gecko advances toward my reflection. Tilting my chin, I open my mouth wide, as if saying 'Ahhh,' such that it will have to crawl right inside it. The gecko inches blithely forward, oblivious. Any moment now it will step into these jaws that it cannot see. That spade-shaped face points like an arrow toward my teeth. I open my jaws a little wider. Pivoting its torso, the gecko lifts its leg and steps. Now, now, it is happening: Godzilla crawls into my mouth, my face, my grave.

Fables

1.

THE BOY BEGS HIS MOTHER TO BUY HIM A BAL-loon. As they leave the grocery store and cross the parking lot, he holds the balloon by a string in his hand. It is round and red, and it bobs a few feet above him. Suddenly his mother looks down and orders him not to release the balloon. Her voice is stern. She says that if he loses it, she will not buy him another. The boy tightens his grip on the string. He had no intention of releasing the balloon. But the mother's prohibition disquiets him, for it seems to be addressed to a specific desire. Her voice implies that she has seen inside him: that deep down—in a place hidden from himself, yet visible to her—he really does want to release the balloon. Otherwise, why bother to forbid it? The boy feels stung by her censure. He grows sullen at the injustice. It isn't fair. He didn't do anything. They approach the car in the parking lot. The day is bright and all the car roofs glint. His fingers fidget, his palm throbs. Before, the balloon had been just a thing that he wanted to hold. Now, he cannot stop thinking about letting it go. He wants to release the string, to spite her. But he knows that this would only prove her right. By forbidding a thought he hadn't had, she has put that thought into his head: now, if he acts on the thought, it will be as good as admitting that he already had it. He glowers up at the balloon. Why had he begged her to buy it in the first place? What had he ever planned on doing with it, if not releasing it? Maybe she was right. For there is now nothing in the world that he more desires—has always desired—than to be rid of this balloon. The boy knows that it is the prohibition that has put this idea into his head, and yet, he cannot remember a time before he had it. It is as if the prohibition has implanted not just the desire, but an entire prehistory of the desire. The second the thought crossed his mind, it had always already been in his mind. The moment his mother spoke to him, he became the boy she was speaking to: the kind of boy who releases balloons, who needs to be told not to. Yes, he imagines that he can remember now: how even in the grocery store—before he had so much as laid eyes on the balloon—even then he was secretly planning to release it. The boy releases the balloon. He watches it rise swiftly and diminish, snaking upward, its redness growing smaller and smaller against the blue sky. His chest hollows out with guilt. He should never have released the balloon. Hearing him whimper, his mother turns to see what has happened. She tells him sharply that she told him not to release the balloon. He begs her to go back into the grocery store and buy him another, but she shakes her head. They are at the car, and she is already digging through her purse for the keys. While she unlocks the door, he takes one last look above him, raking that vast expanse for some fleck of red.

2.

One day at recess, alone behind the jungle gym, the boy spots a crow perched on a low pine branch. He is used to seeing entire flocks in this tree. At dusk dozens will gather together on its branches, visible from across the playground as a cloud of black specks. They dot the treetop then, like ticks in a green flank. Even at that distance he can hear them cawing, a dark sharp sound that they seem to draw from deep within the tree itself, their black bodies growing engorged with it. After school each afternoon, waiting for his mother in the parking lot, the boy will watch them, listening. Today, however, there is only the one crow, and although its beak hangs open, it does not caw. It is perfectly silent. It just sits there, cocking its head and blinking its beady eye in profile. The boy keeps expecting the crow to caw, to let the tree speak through it, in a voice infinitely older than it is. But its beak gapes and no sound comes out. If the boy listens carefully, he can distinguish the rustle of a breeze, some wind in the needles. And then it is possible to imagine that this hissing is emanating from the bird's beak, in steady crackling waves, like static from a broken radio. That is the closest it comes to cawing. Maybe, if he startled it, he could get it to caw, the boy thinks. He kneels at the base of the tree, palming a pinecone from the ground. It is pear-shaped, and imbricated with brown scales, like a grenade of shingles. Rising, he readies the cone at his shoulder, the way a shot-putter would. The crow keeps cocking its head back and forth in its branch. Its beak never narrows. The jaws' twin points remain poised at a precise and unchanging angle, as though biting down on something that the boy can't see: an invisible twig, or tuft of grass. Materials for its nest. The boy waits for the crow to blink, then lobs the pinecone. It misses by a foot, crashing through the foliage and landing behind the tree somewhere. The crow is unfazed. It retracts its head on its neck slightly, but it doesn't caw, and it is careful neither to widen nor narrow its beak. It really is as if there is something in its mouth, something that it is determined not to drop. But its mouth is empty, and so the boy imagines that it is this very emptiness that it is bringing back to its nest: that it is building a nest of absences, gaps. The way it jealously hoards this absence between its mandibles, like a marble. Its beak must be broken, the boy decides, broken open. Or else, no: the bird is simply stubborn. It could caw if it wanted to. It is resisting only to spite him. He gathers four more pinecones. The longer the crow refuses to caw, the louder its silence becomes. The gap in its beak magnifies the stillness around them, until the boy can no longer hear any of the other playground sounds: teachers' whistles; the far-off squawks of his classmates on the soccer field. The boy feels alone with the crow, alone inside this quiet. He hugs the four pinecones against his stomach. He is determined to make the crow caw once before recess is over. He imagines that he is the teacher, the crow his pupil, and he remembers all the ways in which his own teacher calls on him in class: how the boy is made to speak, pronounce new vocabulary terms, say *present* when his name is said. Before recess is over, the boy will make the crow say *present*. He will pelt it with pinecones until it caws, until it con-stitutes itself in a caw, until the moment when—dropping that absence from its beak—the crow will finally present its presence in the present sharpness of its caw. The crow looks up at the sky for a moment. Seizing the opportunity, the boy hurls another of his pinecones, this time missing its torso by a matter of inches. The crow spreads its wings and begins to bate on the branch. For a moment, it almost seems as if it is going to fly away. The boy grips a third pinecone tightly, until its spines bite into his flesh. Soon, he knows, the recess bell will ring. He squints at the crow, focusing its black body in the center of his vision. But just as he is about to throw the pinecone, the bird tucks its neck into its chest, looking down at him. It blinks its black eyes rapidly, agitatedly. Finally it closes its beak. And when at last it caws—rupturing the quiet around them, with a loud, sharp-syllabled *awe*—it is as startling as the first sound in creation.

3.

The boy walks his bike up a hill. In the middle of his street he sees a dead chipmunk, crushed evenly by the tires of a car. It has been flattened into a purse of fur. Around it, a red aura of gore. It makes a brown streak in the center of the lane, straight as a divider line. Ahead of him on the sidewalk he sees a live one. Only a yard away, a second chipmunk stands tensed on all fours, eyeing the boy and his bike. When it wrinkles its nose in rapid sniffs, the boy can tell that it is smelling the carcass stench, wafting in faint off the tarmac behind him. It must seem, to the chipmunk, as if the boy is its brother's murderer. He does not know how to correct this misunderstanding, or reassure the rodent that he means it no harm. He stands silent, trying to stifle any movement that might terrify it. It flees in terror anyway. In an abrupt about-face it dashes up the sidewalk, hugging the hill's concrete retaining wall; when it reaches a ground-level drainpipe—barely bigger than its body—it squeezes inside. The boy walks his bike up to the drainpipe. He moves slowly, so as not to startle the animal. But his wheel spokes make a sinister sound as he approaches: each bony click seems to close in on it, skeleton sound of Death's scythe shaft tapping. When the boy reaches the drainpipe he bends to peer inside. Huddled into a ball, the chipmunk is shaking violently, its walnut-colored chest convulsing. It glares out at the boy, trapped. The rear of the pipe is backed up with gunk: mud, pine needles, dead leaves. The sight of the boy there, darkening the aperture of the drain-pipe, must be a source of unbearable dread for the creature. He starts to back away, but it is too late. Inexplicably, recklessly, the chipmunk rushes forward. It reaches the edge of the pipe and leaps free, landing on the sidewalk at the boy's feet. There it freezes, locking its eyes on his shoes, as if awaiting the killing blow. The boy is careful to stand behind the bike's front tire. He gives the chipmunk a barrier, a zone of safety. He reassures it, by his very posture, that he means it no harm. The chipmunk cow-ers, catching its breath. The wheel casts a barred shadow over its body, a cage of shade in which the chipmunk trembles, frozen amid the many spokes. Indeed, the way that the tire's shadow encloses the rodent, it looks like a phantom hamster wheel. Like the kind of toy Death would keep its pets in—all the mortals who are Death's pets. Maybe that is why the chipmunk dares not move, the boy thinks: because it already understands the nature of this wheel. To flee from Death is just to jog in place. Spinning inside one's dying. The boy takes the bike by the seat and rolls it back. As the front wheel withdraws, the shadow slides off its prisoner. Now the chipmunk is free to flee. But it hunkers to the ground, eyeing the boy's feet with coiled purpose. The boy understands exactly what is about to happen: feeling cornered, the chipmunk will charge him. In a brown blur it will scurry up his shoe and latch onto his pantsleg, the way a squirrel mounts a tree trunk. As it claws at his pants for purchase, tearing through the cotton, the boy will be able to feel its bark-sharpened nails get a scansorial grip into his shinbone. The sear of skin tearing; the beading of blood. He cannot help imagining all this. He will kick out his leg—as if it were aflame, he imagines—but the chipmunk will hold fast to him, out of rabidness perhaps. Then the boy will have no choice. Above all, he knows, he will have to keep the creature from biting him. After trying so hard not to frighten it, he will be forced to kill it. With his free foot he will have to scrape it from his pantsleg, onto the sidewalk, and stomp the life out of it, flattening it as dispassionately as that car had flattened the rodent in the road. In this way, he will become everything the animal mistook him for: its murderer, its personal death. The boy stares down at the chipmunk, which has begun to vibrate like a revving engine. Because it was wrong about the boy, it will prove to be right about the boy. Because it has mistaken the boy for a murderer, it will make the boy murder it. And so perhaps, the boy reflects, the chipmunk wasn't wrong after all: maybe it could see clearly what the boy could not. That he had a role to play in its fate. The boy stomps his foot lightly on the sidewalk. Still the chipmunk does not run. It is ready now. It must have been waiting for this moment its entire life. Seeing the boy today, it recognized him instantaneously: he was the human who had been set aside for it, the boy it had been assigned from the beginning. *He* was the place it was fated to die. Now, at long last, it has an appointment to keep.

4.

On his walk home from school the boy pauses at the edge of his neighbors' yard. It is wide and well manicured and unfenced, and today their dog is out in it. A standard chocolate poodle—as tall as the boy's chest when standing—it is couchant now, in the middle of the lawn. It has not yet noticed the boy from where it lies. It pants happily in the midday heat, its long tongue lolling from its jaw. Some curls are combed into a bouffant on its forehead, where they seem to seethe, massed and wrinkled like an exposed brown brain. The dog's owners—the boy's neighbors—are nowhere to be seen. Far out of earshot, deep within their white two-story house. If the dog were to suddenly bark loudly and attack the boy—if the boy were to shout for help—they would not be able to hear. At least twice a week the boy passes the poodle in the yard like this. The sight of it always paralyzes him with fear. He will stop walking for a moment, then sidle slowly down the sidewalk, careful not to draw the dog's attention. What is to keep it from mauling him? The owners are never outside with it. Evidently they trust the poodle. It is allowed to roam unsupervised in the yard, which is not technically—but only appears to be—unfenced. In reality, the boy's mother has explained to him, it employs a so-called invisible fence: a virtual boundary of radio waves tracing the perimeter of the lawn. GPS coordinates are broadcast to the dog's shock collar, which is programmed to administer mild jolts of admonitory electricity whenever the poodle trespasses the property line. There is nothing—she reassured him—to be afraid of. After a few hours of behavioral training, the dog would have learned to obey the dictates of its collar. It would have internalized the limits of its prison. And so even if it noticed the boy one day— even if it bounded barking toward him—it would know to stop short at the pavement. As his mother was explaining this, the boy nodded to show he understood. But deep down he still does not trust the invisible fence. He wonders, for instance, how it is supposed to keep other animals *out* of the yard. All it would take is for a rabid bat, or raccoon, or chipmunk, to crawl across the boundary line and bite and infect the dog. Then when the boy was walking home one day, he would see the poodle foaming at the mouth in the yard, with nothing but a symbolic cage of X/Y coordinates separating it from him. And what was to keep the dog—mindless with rage—from simply disregarding the fence, in that case? Assuming it could remember the fence at all. For the rabies may very well have wiped its memory clean, erasing its behavioral training. Then the dog would be incapable of recognizing symbolic cages, only real ones, and it would not think twice before bounding across the yard at the boy. He stares at the poodle. It is facing the house, panting. He does not know its name. Sometimes he imagines being attacked by the dog, and in these fantasies—which he indulges in involuntarily, standing motionless with fear on the sidewalk—he assigns it the name Gerald. He imagines the neighbors running across the lawn, calling *Gerald, Gerald, get off him*, even as the poodle pins him to the pavement and snaps its jaws. This is always the most horrifying moment, for the boy, in the fantasy. How the dog can ignore its own name. How it can conduct this beast's balancing act, suspended between two minds: the mind that answers to Gerald and the mind that murders meat. For once it starts tearing into the boy's throat, it is not Gerald any longer: it has already regressed, passed backward through some baptism. Not only nameless now, but unnamable. That is what terrifies the boy. The name cannot enclose the dog forever. It is just a kind of kennel you can keep it in. The boy pictures all the flimsy walls of this poodle's name: the collar's silver tag, engraved *Gerald*; the blue plastic food bowl, marked *Gerald*; the sound of its owners' voices, shouting *Gerald*. Each of them is just another invisible fence, which the dog can choose to trespass at will. The poodle turns to him now, cocking its head sideways. At any moment, the boy knows, the animal could transform from a friendly housepet into a ferocious guardian: a Cerberus at the gates of the hell that it will make this boy's life, if he makes even one move toward its masters. From his place on the sidewalk, the boy reaches out his arm. He extends it over the lawn, as over a candle's flame. Unfolding his hand, he holds it palm-down inside the dog's territory. The poodle rises, stretching its hind legs and shaking the tiredness from its coat. It begins to cross the yard. Every few steps it stops, eyeing the boy. *It* is afraid of *him*, he realizes. The dog must recognize the threat that the boy poses. That he could snap. Attack it. That he is wild, unpredictable, unconstrained. From the poodle's point of view, the only thing holding the boy back is a kind of invisible fence, or else system of invisible fences. The name his mother gave him. The school uniform he wears. The fact that he walks with his back straight, and hair combed, and that he knows better than to murder his neighbors' pets. This is all that protects the poodle from him now, the poodle must be thinking. He imagines himself enraged like the dog, rabid like the dog; he imagines himself punching the animal, in blind mindlessness. Yes, it is possible. He can see himself that way, one day: suspended over a void where no name reaches. The dog approaches the edge of the grass. It stops a foot back, looking up at the boy's hand. Suspicious, it sniffs. It curls back its lip slightly, revealing a white incisor. The boy's palm is cold with sweat. It is exactly as he always imagined. He wants to call the dog's name, in soothing tones—*There, Gerald. There, Gerald*—but he remembers that *Gerald* is not its real name. And so, not knowing what to call it, the boy says nothing. He stands there on the pavement. The dog stands on the grass.

5.

Behind his house one afternoon the boy finds a chunk of ice. It is lying on the sidewalk, fist-sized and flecked with dirt. Someone must have dropped it there from a five-pound bag or a cooler. Now it lies exposed to the summer. It is the clear kind, blue-gray all the way through, except at its core, where a brilliant whiteness has condensed: sunlight, locked inside. Tiny hairlines of trapped light radiate outward, veining the ice's interior from corner to corner, touching the edges and returning to center. The radiance seems to ricochet around in there, bouncing off the walls of its container. Even as the boy is considering this, the ice jerks toward him. The chunk shifts a centimeter across the pavement, then stops abruptly, as if thinking better of it. The boy can hardly stifle his surprise. He knows that there is some kind of glacial principle at work: that as the chunk melts, it lubricates its own passage, and is displaced across the pavement in a basal slide. But still, the way it had moved. Exactly like a living thing. Bending down, he can see the darkened trail behind the ice, where it has wet the pebbled concrete. While the boy is studying this, the chunk scrapes forward again, another centimeter. The light at its center glints, melting it from within. Where is it headed? The boy's shadow stops an inch or two away, and it almost seems as if the ice is trying to crawl inside. As if, stuck beneath the sun, it is seeking shelter in his shade. Dragging itself into his shadow. And it's strange, too, the boy thinks, how what melts it helps it move. That is the paradox the ice has been presented with: this light at its core, the light that is killing it, is what enables it to escape. It has to glide along a film of its own dying. The faster that it moves, the more of itself that it melts, and so it is alive with its own limit, animated by this horizon inscribed in its being. There is a lesson to be learned in this, the boy thinks. He watches the chunk, waiting for it to judder forward again. The ball of light sits calmly at its center, like a pilot in the cockpit. It will steer the chunk forward by destroying it. Death is what's driving the ice. It collaborates with the ice's other side, the side that wants to survive, and together these twin engines propel the chunk to safety. As the boy watches, a thread of water melts off one edge, trickling down the sidewalk in an exploratory rivulet. Paving the way for the glacier. The boy was right: it is headed directly for him. He watches the tendril inch into the shadow of his head, worming blindly forward. It punches deeper and deeper into the darkness. This is the track that the death-driven ice will travel, the boy understands. Gradually the glacier will slide into his head. One-way into the shade. One-way into the shadow that his skull casts. There has to be some kind of lesson in this.

Za

TWO WEEKS AFTER B LEAVES, A RECEIVES HER first email from him. In it, he describes the various people he has met abroad so far. He makes no explicit mention of lovers. But he devotes an entire page to recounting a group Scrabble game, with particular attention paid to the woman seated next to him. Ever since receiving the email (one a.m., perhaps a reasonable hour where he is), A has not left her laptop. She has already reread the letter several times. She is trying to understand what it means.

A met B only a month before he left. She knew from the outset that this trip was imminent. He had hidden nothing. My work will be sending me away soon, he had told her: Six weeks. And what about this, she had asked, referring to the bed in which they lay. No one else, he promised, if that is what you want. And she had said: You don't have to do that for me.

It is difficult to tell, from this email, whether he has kept his promise. Instead of addressing the promise directly, he meticulously describes the Scrabble game, almost play-by-play. A could not care less about B's Scrabble game. She wants to know whether he has met anyone else. He appears to have met this woman. Yet it is difficult to tell, from B's description, who she is, or what she means.

She's just a colleague, B wrote, another American from the company, as well as the most aggravating Scrabble player he has ever encountered. She was the kind of player who contested every recherché two- or three-letter word on the board, B wrote. For instance, on one of B's very first turns, he played *jo* horizontally, scoring a triple-letter on the *j*. Since he had set the *j* atop a vertical word—*ape*, forming *jape*—he scored a second triple-letter. The *o*, too, was a vertical addition: he'd placed it on *bi*, forming *obi*. The play was worth more than fifty points. But the woman—this woman—challenged all three of B's words. She had never heard of any of them, she scoffed, B wrote. She challenged *jape*, so he looked it up (they hadn't brought a dictionary; he had to search Hasbro.com's Scrabble page on his smart phone). *Jape*: to joke or quip, to make sport of. She challenged *jo*, so he looked it up: an Irish term of endearment, a sweetheart. She challenged *obi*, so he looked it up: an alternative spelling of *obeah*, a religious system of African origin, involving witchcraft and sorcery. The whole ordeal lasted fifteen minutes, B wrote. The reception at the compound was capricious, so the Hasbro website kept lagging. At one point B even had to hold his phone above his head—squinting to see the 4G signal's ziggurat of blue bars—until finally *obi*'s page had loaded. In the end, of course, the woman's challenges came to nothing. But because it was a friendly game, informal, no one made her forfeit her turn.

Naturally A had not meant what she had said, when they were lying together in bed. It had been a gambit on her part. She had said, You don't have to do that for me, when what she wanted more than anything was for him to do that for her. Yet there were limits to what or how she could ask. Obviously she could not request his fidelity outright. She would be overstepping her prerogatives as his lover. They had been together only for a matter of weeks, and while she might have drawn future credit on the relationship, she would have risked jinxing the relationship. What's more, she might have come across as presumptuous, possessive, jealous; and if she made him feel at all claustrophobic, he was liable to take up a lover on principle (whether or not he even realized—consciously—that that was what he was doing).

On the other hand, her current stratagem was not without its own risks. Namely, that B would take her at her word: that he would pursue a lover, or lovers, without guilt, because that was what she had encouraged. But she trusted B not to take her at her word. He was smart enough, she knew, to detect the double meaning in her message: *You don't have to do that for me* meant *Please do this for me*. In this way, her so-called permission put B at a moral disadvantage: because he was free to pursue lovers, it was out of the question for him to pursue lovers; because there was no need to feel disloyal (for he had every right), he would succeed only in feeling selfish (for exploiting those rights). That was the double bind A had placed him in. She knew this, and she knew that B knew this. What she did not know—what she could not determine—was whether B knew she knew. Because for the stratagem to work, it must not seem like a stratagem. A had to seem undesigning, self-sacrificing; her position had to seem like a plea, as opposed to a ploy. Only then would B feel tenderness toward her, and make it a point of pride to remain faithful. His constancy would even take on an erotic quality: he would derive pleasure from denying himself pleasure. Whereas if he ever suspected that she was playing on his feelings—that *she* was the one denying him pleasure—he would begin to feel claustrophobic. Then they would be back at square one. It was all a matter of how many moves ahead B thought A was thinking.

However matters stand now, B's email gives nothing away. Whether he has met someone else, or hasn't—it does not say. It is almost conspicuously indirect. It is as if he is trying to tell her something, by not telling her anything. That description of the Scrabble game is so long, and so beside the point, that it has to be making some kind of hidden point. For example, the detail about the cell-phone coverage. Why had he included it? Was this the reason he hadn't called? And his caricature of the woman. She is the only player at the table whom he bothers to describe in any detail. But why? Why, after a two-week silence, write to A about her?

If A takes the email at its word, the woman is nothing more than a bête noire of B's. He had found her amusing, and was describing her to amuse A. Throughout the game, B wrote, the woman kept pouting about *jo* and *obi*. There was no point in playing, she would pout, because B had already demolished them all, right out of the gate. She grew increasingly petulant, especially when it became clear to her that—among the four players—she had by far the lowest score, irrecoverably low. Do I really have to keep playing, she would ask. Oops, she would say, feigning to drop her beige tiles on the carpet, but in fact scattering them everywhere like a child. Things came to a head toward the end of the game, B wrote, when B—in the lead now by dozens of points—played *za* (the latest addition, evidently, to the Scrabble dictionary: slang for *pizza*). The woman had a field day over *za*. *Za?!*, she shrieked, B wrote. *What is* za?! *Za* is a word, B assured her: he could look it up in the Scrabble dictionary, if she wanted. But by this time the woman had had quite enough of the Scrabble dictionary. She did not bother challenging *za*. For the remainder of the game, she simply kept exclaiming to herself, at random: *I still can't get over* za!

A is disinclined to take B's email at its word. Over and above his caricature of the woman, there is something B wants A to know. For one thing, A does not like the sound of all this pouting. It sounds to A as if the woman was flirting with B. Each indignant outburst seems to bear a double message: *You cheat, you play fake words* means *You know such esoteric words. You demolished all of us* means *Your vocabulary ravishes me.* B was not an idiot. Surely he was alert to these flirtations. But if he was alert to them, then why had he included them? Why had he sent them for A to read?

Perhaps B thought nothing of it, or thought that A would think nothing of it. Or perhaps he knew that the anecdote would make her jealous, and had included it to let her know that strange women were flirting with him. Conversely, the anecdote might have been designed to allay her jealousy, and to reassure her: B might have been demonstrating his fidelity by skewering his would-be suitors.

And there is another interpretation, too, A realizes: that the person B is reassuring is, not A, but himself. For it is always possible that he is skewering the woman for his own sake. If B had initially been attracted to her, and even considered pursuing her, then he might have felt pangs of guilt at some point during the Scrabble game. Out of remorse, he would have begun to resent the woman, and it would be for this reason—to atone for his mental or emotional infidelity—that he would have caricatured her so mercilessly, picking her apart, destroying her, then bringing her remains to A's doorstep, with an almost feline fealty, like some bird he had slain.

Of course, if this were the case, then B would doubtless be aware of what he was doing. At every step, the psychodynamics would be transparent to him. No component of the process (the guilt, the atonement, the reconciliatory spectacle of the caricature) would operate unconsciously. And if the psychodynamics were transparent to B, then he had to know that they would be transparent to A. Which left her with the same question, at the same impasse: why had he included the description in the first place? Either to make her jealous, to let her know that he was attracted to women there; or to reassure her, to demonstrate his fidelity by repenting for that attraction.

Each time A rereads the email, B's remarks about the woman seem less and less straightforward. Toward the end of his description of her, he makes a comment that consistently mystifies A: he had found the woman so deeply annoying, he wrote, that he began to imagine how awful it would be to be married to her. He fantasized about the passive-aggressive punishments he would have to concoct for her, whenever they were driving home from Scrabble games like this one. *Za?*, he would ask her, laughing bitterly to himself at the steering wheel, B wrote: You can't get over *za*?

A cannot stop returning to this section of the email. Why bring up marriage? What was he trying to imply? For whatever reason, B wanted A to imagine him married to this woman: driving her home, climbing into bed. Or else he wanted A to imagine him imagining himself married to this woman. It amounts to the same, either way: he is letting A know that he finds this woman, not only attractive, but marriageable. Marriage had entered his mind. Were it not for her Scrabble comportment, B might have made her his bride. That is what B wants A to be thinking—what he designed his email to make A think—A thinks.

Unless—and this is also a possibility—A is misreading that comment. Unless the marriage that B was hinting at is, not with this woman, but rather with A. Then the comment would have an utterly different subtext: B would be preparing A for the kind of lover he is, for when he returns home. If you ever behave this petulantly in public, he would be warning her, you can expect passive-aggressiveness in return.

A has to think. A has to think this through. But all that A can think about is B in bed with this woman. B is betraying A with this woman, and out of guilt he has embedded a confession in his email. Or maybe he feels no guilt, because there is no betrayal. A gave him, after all, her permission. Or maybe B is not sleeping with the woman, but still wants A to think he is. Maybe he saw straight through A's so-called permission—recognizing it for the ploy that it was—and is punishing her for it. Who is to say that he hasn't fabricated this entire email, concocting the Scrabble game out of whole cloth, simply to make A jealous? Perhaps this is just the kind of passive-aggressive punishment B had in mind. Now A begins to doubt that there ever was a Scrabble game, or else—if there had in fact been a Scrabble game—that this woman really existed, or else—if this woman indeed existed—that she had behaved so flirtatiously, challenging all of B's words, or else—if she did happen to challenge all or some of B's words—that *these* were the words. The words were too apposite to be real words. Clearly B was winking at her with these words: it was all a joke (a *jape*), A was still his sweetheart (his *jo*), he was just casting a spell over her, a little bit of witchcraft (*obi*) to make her jealous.

On the one hand, she knows that she is reading too much into the email. But on the other hand, she knows that she can never read too much into B's emails. In matters of love, they had both agreed, it is impossible to read too much into anything. This was one of the first conversations they had had together. Being in love, they had agreed in bed one night, meant being in a state of interpretive hysteria. Every detail was significant, polysemous, charged. That was why lovers had to be especially careful with one another, so as not to arouse suspicions. No literary critic in the world, B had claimed, was more vigilant than a suspicious lover. There was a kind of close-reading involved in cuckoldry. There was a whole hermeneutics of cuckoldry. The domestic space became alive with signs. If a wife came home at the wrong hour, in the wrong dress, by the wrong door, if she used a word she had never used before—the husband would notice. Where had she been? Who had taught her that word? If she started mentioning a colleague she had never mentioned, or stopped mentioning a colleague she used to always mention, or suddenly began rereading *Madame Bovary*, *Lady Chatterley's Lover*, 'The Kreutzer Sonata': these were all signs. If she so much as put on Beethoven's *Kreutzer Sonata* before dinner, that, too, constituted a sign. In each case the husband would ask himself: What does this mean? What was she trying to tell him?

So B would be expecting A to read into this email. He would have had that conversation in mind while writing it. When he mentioned the cell-phone coverage, the woman, their marriage—he would have known. When he neglected to mention the promise that they had made one another, he had to know that this omission would be more conspicuous—more charged with meaning—than the actual content of his letter. And it was likely for the same reason that he had not asked *her* about the promise. In deliberately refraining from asking whether she had met anyone, he was trying to tell her something.

The absence of this question is the worst aspect of the email by far. Why didn't he ask? She doesn't know what to make of it. The implications are endless. It is like a blank Scrabble tile that A has been given, a wall of inscrutable smooth beige, onto which she can project any meaning whatsoever. Depending on what value she assigns it, the question's absence could mean (could be made to mean) any number of things: that B trusts her; that B wants her to *think* that he trusts her; that B respects her privacy and autonomy (or wants her to think he does); that B is incurious, indifferent, could not care less whether she is seeing anyone (or wants her to think that he is); that B is, on the contrary, overly curious, jealous even, obsessed with the prospect of her seeing someone, but dreads ever actually asking her; or, finally, that B is simply delimiting the perimeter of their discourse, since by neglecting to ask A this question, he is as good as saying to her, 'Never ask me this question,' 'We are not allowed to ask each other this question,' 'This question is banned from play.'

If only B had asked the question, A thinks. Even in jest. Then A would be able to ask the question in return. But now she will never be able to ask the question. Unless she wants to be the first of them to break down and ask the question, she will have to somehow trap B into asking the question. And perhaps, A realizes, that is B's tactic as well: perhaps he devised this description of the woman as bait for A, merely to provoke A into asking the question, so that B, in his follow-up email, could ask the question himself, without forfeiting his advantage or losing any face. Of course, two could always play at that game. A could deflect B's stratagem, either by ignoring B's Scrabble anecdote altogether, or else by responding to it with good-natured aplomb, with none of the expected jealousy. She could even commend his caricature of the woman: 'How hilarious,' she could write, 'tell me more about your marriage fantasy.' If deployed properly, A's display of supreme indifference might rattle B into asking the question ('Why doesn't she care? Is *she* seeing someone?'). A would have reversed B's own stratagem, turning it instantly against him, just as a Scrabble player can pluralize an opponent's word, tacking an *s* onto it and siphoning its points.

However A chooses to respond, one thing is certain: she must not reveal her suspicions about the woman. The last thing in the world she can write is, 'Are you seeing this woman?', or even, 'Do you find this woman attractive?' Such questions are sure to make B feel claustrophobic. Besides which, A would only be giving B ideas. If B wasn't attracted to this woman already, A's prying would surely put the thought into his head, inspiring him to pay closer attention in the future ('*Am* I attracted to her?'). Then it would only be a matter of time before they slept together. That is the problem with jealousy, A thinks: it always ends by engendering the thing it dreads. By obsessing over your lover's colleague ('Are you attracted to her?'; 'Was *she* at this party?'; 'Did you email her?'), you only brainwash your lover into obsessing over his colleague. Although you had intended to repel your lover from the colleague, you end up driving your lover straight into the arms of the colleague. 'It's funny,' your lover might confide to the colleague one day, 'but she thinks we're having an affair.' 'That *is* funny,' the colleague might say, and then it is all over. Now the idea has taken on a life of its own. It is entirely too late to stop it. That is the prophetic power of jealousy, A thinks: it is eventually self-fulfilling, given a long enough period of time; it has a sibylline effect on the libido. You keep on telling the lover that he is doomed to sleep with the colleague, and he keeps on denying it with blind vehemence, until the day when finally your barrage of insistences and suspicions and auguries penetrates through to his unconscious, catalyzing an anagnorisis in him: then he is able to look at the colleague anew, noticing for the first time how beautiful she is, and he recognizes her at last as the woman with whom he is fated to betray you.

A starts to reread B's email. It is now two a.m. Soon, she knows, she will have to write B back. And she will need to exercise maximum caution when choosing her words. She thinks through all her options, all the questions she can ask or neglect to ask: about the Scrabble game, the woman, the cell phone. She rearranges the possibilities in her mind. She does not need to solve every problem now: once she emails, he will have to email back. That will give her another opportunity to respond, and then it will be his turn, and so on for the next four weeks, until he comes home. There will still be time for several more rounds, she reassures herself, as she types *Dear B* into the reply box.

A Premonition

IT WAS LATE AND I WAS BESET BY A BLACK WIND. I ducked into a costume store, the only business open at that hour. Inside I was glad to be warm, but the old man behind the counter looked me over suspiciously. There were slick dead leaves plastered to my greatcoat; beyond the shopwindow, trees whipped violently in the wind. I pretended to interest myself in the racks of masks. The racks were arranged in rows: rubbery faces, loose as flayed skin, hung from their hooks like clothing. The faces were frozen in dreadful expressions. I handled one after another. They were clammy to touch, and left a faint chemical smell on my fingers. Some were monsters, others the victims of monsters. Some had blades buried in their heads, for instance. None had eyes, only dark holes, ovals cut out of the latex. These, I understood, were where my own eyes would peer out from the mask. I took down three monsters of a species that I didn't recognize. Two were hairy, with indeterminate snouts. They didn't bare their teeth. Their ears were sharp, as if they could hear shrill sounds from far distances. The third was recognizably a man's face, except totally white and hairless, and where its mouth should be, a seal of flesh. I brought them over to the old man at the counter. 'And these?' I said. 'They are the souls of thieves,' he said. Immediately I let out a loud laugh. But when the old man did not smile, I realized that he had been serious: I was holding the souls of thieves, these flimsy weights in my hands. Shoplifters who had been caught by the old man and transformed into terrible masks. 'That's fine,' I said. I placed a bill from my pocket down on the counter, in fact the only bill I had—it was more than I could afford, but no matter. I slipped the white-faced mask over my head and left the other two on the counter with the old man, then departed from the shop still wearing the mask. I felt fine. Outside, the thief's soul protected my face from the wind. My breath was trapped inside it, and my face grew quite hot even. Walking home I felt my neck dampen with sweat. Through the thief's ragged eyeholes, everything that I saw was an ill-gotten good: the empty streets were mine, and lampposts mine; the dark clouds, too, dissolving off the moon like smoke, they were mine, and the moonlight mine, and the gleaming backs of leaves as the trees whipped. I stole a glance of the river N—, of the bridge rail, I stole a glance of my own hand. There was a great greediness in my looking. At the end of my street, still several blocks off from my house, I paused before a thick tree that I had never noticed before. It was short, not much taller than I, but it held its branches out wide, and they were heavy with leaves black as midnight. I peeled the mask from my head and propped it on the foliage. Its white face sagged, and I could tell that it would fall to the ground. Carefully I worked a branch up through the neckline of the mask, positioning one of its tridents of twigs inside the cavity of the nose. When the mask was secure I stepped back. A wind started in, and the tree swayed. Swaying also in its field of leaves was that white face, bobbing up and down with its branch, like a piece of trash on black water. It even became possible to regard the tree as a creature of fur, out of whose dark pelt a human face leered. 'There,' I said, feeling the tree's gaze on me. 'There, there.' In the wind the tree whipped more violently, like an animal heaving itself against the bars of its cage, and I no longer felt safe in its presence. My heart beat hard, I had difficulty breathing. As the leaves roiled, the white face tossed around in the foliage, rearing in what seemed like frenzy, and the whole time it kept its gaze on me. Finally I had to avert my eyes, for in that moment I understood. Everything grew clear, as in a premonition. This was the angel that Death would send for me.

Radical Closure

TODAY YOU TRY WRITING OUTSIDE YOUR APART-
ment. You walk to a small neighborhood café, order an iced coffee, and take a seat at one of the wrought-iron tables on the
covered deck. You can tell at once that it is not an ideal writing
space: there are no power outlets, and the conversations at the
tables around you are loud. But earlier, when you made the decision to come here, you reasoned that you would be more pro-
ductive in a public space. Above all else, you told yourself, you
had to get out of the apartment. For the past few days you had
locked yourself inside, and you had not written a single word.
Now the apartment was too haunted by your failures—too
haunted, in a word, by self-hatred—and you already knew how
a work session would progress at your desk. After opening your
laptop to the blank document, you would stare at the screen for
hours, possessed by the same thoughts that you had been thinking every day. Idiot, you would think. Failure. These were the
thoughts that haunted your apartment. You could not sit down
at your desk without thinking them. Just as a ghost, you imagine,
must repeat its dying words for eternity, so too were you doomed
to repeat these thoughts. It was as if some part of you had died
at your desk, and now you were the ghost of that moment. If
you tried writing there today, you knew, your mind would simply
pick up where it left off yesterday: caught like a specter inside
this eternal loop or hesternal circuit. No, the apartment was out
of the question. Whereas the café, you told yourself, was an un-

habituated space: you had never worked there before, had never developed any previous patterns of thought, positive or negative, and so it was possible that the shock of its novelty would defamiliarize the blank document, allowing you to write at least one paragraph. And even if you failed to write, you reasoned, it might be refreshing to fail in new surroundings. You had to get out of the apartment. You had to leave that suffocating structure behind. But now—as you open your laptop to the blank document and take the first sip from your glass of iced coffee— you understand that you have left nothing behind. Idiot, you think. Failure. The self-hatred is as strong here as ever. You are thinking the exact same thoughts here as you would have been thinking at your desk. And so it is as if, you reflect, some part of you still *is* at your desk. As if, while your body is at the café, your mind has remained behind in the apartment. Thinking its apartment thoughts. You should have known that it would not be so easy to escape. Your mistake lay in conflating the apartment with its physical dimensions: its walls and hallways, the thousand square feet that it occupies in space. In addition to these, you realize, the apartment must possess something like *psychological* dimensions, a state of mind that you generate around yourself. Over and above the apartment structure is the apartment construct, a zone of influence or domed logic which, encompassing your body, follows you wherever you go. Looked at in this way, it is less that the apartment is haunted than that you are haunted by the apartment. For from the point of view of a ghost, that is precisely what haunting means: while a mortal tenant is free to leave at any time, a ghost is bound to the premises eternally. Even if the house is demolished, the ghost will go on haunting its grounds. And if a skyscraper is built in its place, the ghost will haunt the skyscraper, wandering down its hallways and its stairwells *as if* they are its house. Transpose the ghost's bones to a new burial ground, on the opposite side of the world, and it will persist in haunting its new graveyard, behaving in all things—in all places—as if it is still inside its house. The house is its haunt, which means that it is haunted by the house. Everywhere it goes *is* the house. Even when crossing a misty field, or a hotel lobby, the ghost is still walking down the hardwood hallway that it died in: all it sees are the fringed rugs beneath its feet, the crystal chandeliers above it. While the physical structure of the mansion may have burned to the ground centuries ago, the mental structure lives on as a spectral projection. Wherever the ghost finds itself, this bygone mansion's hallways and chambers will radiate out from its regenerating body, like a system of hardwood starfish arms. That is how things stand with you and the apartment. Recalling now the lightness you felt this morning, as you stepped out into the sunshine and locked the front door behind you, you are filled with disgust. You were a fool. It was no use fleeing the physical apartment when you were still immured in the mental apartment. Exiting the physical front door brought you no nearer the mental front door. Every block you walked toward the café—every step you took away from the physical hallways—only led you deeper into the maze of the mental hallways. And at the end of the day, whenever you leave the café, the five blocks you will have to walk back to your physical apartment—the half-mile of oak-shaded concrete leading straight to the physical apartment—will all still be *inside the mental apartment.* You can never breach those mental walls. That is the true philosophical paradox: not how you can travel from point A to point B without first traversing a spatial infinity, bridging all the subdivisible points between them; but rather, how you can travel from *mind A* to *mind B* without first traversing a *psychological* infinity. Leaving the apartment in one frame of mind, how could you ever arrive at a new one? Between what you are thinking now and what you would like to think, there are a billion thoughts—a billion iterations of *Idiot* and *Failure*—that you first have to pass through. You begin gulping the iced coffee, stifling the urge to flee the café. There is nowhere you can go. Even if you went to the farthest library, you would still be trapped in your apartment consciousness. Even if you boarded a plane to fly across the country—across the world—you would manage to transform the passenger cabin into your apartment. You experience a fleeting vision of yourself on the moon, sitting cross-legged with your laptop alone in that white wasteland, and it is an image not of escape but of imprisonment. Even there, you understand, you would be in your apartment: the moment you set foot on its lunar surface, it would become an apartment moon, a one-bedroom moon, its cratered landscape carpeted over with your apartment's carpet. No, you think, finishing the iced coffee and drumming one foot against the deck. The moon is not far enough because nowhere is far enough. There is no minimum physical distance you can travel that will suffice to access an outside. There is no apartness from your apartment now. *Everywhere* is your apartment. The apartment is involute, endless, all perimeter: a kind of radical closure. Even when you are outside it, you are inside it, because *it* is inside *you*. You have internalized its thousand square feet of space, and now, wherever you go, you are there. The bedroom. The living room. The kitchen. Like any ghost, haunted by this space that you died in, you are halfway between a hermit crab and a hologram: the apartment is both the shell you carry around yourself and the spectral image you project onto all your surroundings. Your heart starts pounding at this thought, and you look around you at the café courtyard, at this *so-called café courtyard*. Darting your eyes from left to right, you survey the scene for any evidence that you have actually left your apartment. There are other patrons sitting at the wrought-iron tables, lifting white demitasses from white dishes; there is a finch perched on the splintered banister, regarding you with an eye as impassive and black as a security camera; there is a grass-green anole crawling across one of the planks of the deck, its head raised as if tracking prey; there are ashtrays; there are palm trees and chairs, dead leaves on the ground, you are to all outward appearances sitting in the courtyard of a neighborhood café, but still, nevertheless, you can just make out—flickering transparently over everything—the image of your bed, your desk, your bookcase. You never left, you think, pushing the empty glass away from you. You never succeeded—not even for a second—in getting out from under the ceiling of your apartment. It will always be like this, you think. It will always be like this. As if in despair, your laptop screen goes dark with sleep, and you do not move a finger to the keyboard to wake it. You stare beyond the dull screen, down to the deck, where the anole is still crawling forward, making slow progress. It looks from left to right guiltily as it advances. It seems to be heading for a dead leaf lying a few feet away: the deck is littered with crisp brown discards from the vines threading the trellis overhead, and you watch as the lizard closes in on—then crawls on top of—this one. Its toes grip the papery surface. Once it has established its fourfold foothold it pauses, standing perfectly still. Its body tenses, as if every pore in its pebbled skin were a straining ear, listening. And then that green skin begins to fade. For a moment you assume that a shadow has passed over its body, the way that the air will dim when a cloud crosses the sun. But soon you see that the lizard is changing colors: its skin yellows at first, then descends through gradations of brown, until finally—after having slowly darkened through bark tones and the pale beige of wood chips—it reaches the exact same shade as the leaf. In the space of a few seconds, the lizard has traversed the color spectrum of two seasons: it has crossed that chromatophoric infinity, passing from green to brown just as—in the preceding months—the leaf had. The lizard has synthesized September in its skin. You cannot stop staring at the lizard. Was that what your brain looked like, you wonder, as it learned to mimic the mental apartment? While you sat perfectly still at your desk, did your brain embrown like this, blending gradually with its surroundings, flushing itself with darker and darker thoughts until, in the end, you could barely distinguish your apartment-colored consciousness from your apartment? The lizard, too, has grown indistinguishable. You can still make it out on the leaf, but you know that if you had not been watching this entire time—if you had just arrived in the courtyard and glanced down at the deck—your gaze would have swept across the floor without registering it. It has merged that completely with the dead leaf. Its body has all but disappeared into the deadness, grown invisible against a background of brown decay. It is, you imagine, a form of ontological camouflage, no different from a possum's playing dead. The anole is disguising itself from predators by absenting itself altogether from the world of predators and prey, of beings and being, retreating instead into the nonbeing beneath the leaf. Maybe, you imagine, that is why it had to pause there so long, with such concentration: maybe it had to draw the death out of the leaf, absorbing autumnal energies into its body, growing brown from this bloodmeal the way that a mosquito's belly will redden as it drinks. By standing on the leaf, you think, the lizard is drilling down into death. The leaf is just the visible vein of that invisible world. And at this thought you suddenly want—you do not know how—to warn the lizard. *Do not do that*, you want to tell it. *Do anything but that.* For you know, as the reptile does not, what the price of entering a radical closure is. Like a ghost in its house, or like you in your apartment, the lizard will soon become an eternal tenant: having partaken of the death of the leaf and therefore died before dying on the leaf—having entered, even for a second, the brown house of the leaf—the lizard will never be able to leave. Everywhere it goes, it will still be deep inside it. Indeed, even as you are thinking this—even as you drum your foot hard against the deck, to scare the lizard away—you see that it is already too late. For although the lizard does scurry across the deck in fear, its body remains exactly as brown as before, retaining the leaf's shade: its body has left the leaf—all four feet have departed from its surface—but its mind remains behind, still enmeshed in that brown logic. Every cell of its skin still thinking leaf thoughts. You watch it dart off the deck and disappear into the shrubs beyond, where, surrounded by green grasses, its brown body will prove a liability, a provocation of conspicuity to the birds that prey in the courtyard, perhaps even to the finch that, you see now, has vanished from the banister. Yes. The lizard is still inside the leaf, and it may very well die there: while trapped beneath the finch's talons, you imagine, while being crushed in the bird's beak, the brown lizard will still be inside the brown leaf. Not even death is an escape, you think, rising from the table and packing your laptop back into your bag. Exiting the courtyard, you begin the long walk back to your apartment. Not even death is an outside for the dead.

White Dialogues

LISTEN TO HER, BEREYTER SAYS, AS TOGETHER WE
watch the mute woman mouthing something on the screen. On
the pull-down canvas behind him, a single scene from Alfred
Hitchcock's *Vertigo* repeats itself on a loop. Earlier this semester,
the fall of what is to be my final year at the University, Bereyter
accepted our cinema department's prestigious postdoctoral fel-
lowship, to continue his so-called groundbreaking work on *white
dialogues*. Now, several months later, on a dismal morning in No-
vember, he is delivering a lecture on the progress of his research,
addressing a scattered audience of roughly twenty people—hu-
manities majors, graduate students, our fellow film colleagues—
from a walnut lectern at the front of the darkened seminar

room, down here in the basement of the historic Wolfsegg Hall. Bereyter, still in his late twenties, is a natty dresser, and for the occasion he is wearing a bone-white oxford button-down with a navy cable-knit cardigan, a prep-school ensemble that only serves to reinforce his precocity. That is the brazen boy-genius image he means to project: so young, and yet already he has (in his own terms) fashioned a brand-new technique of close reading, or else has (as my colleagues in the cinema department have put it) *blown film scholarship wide open*. I am sitting alone in the back row, in one of the room's uncomfortable desk chairs, with their stiff polypropylene seats and claustrophobic tablet arms. I have laid an opened notebook and two pens on the desktop, even though note-taking will be impossible. The single light source in the room is the overhead projector, a rectangular turret mounted directly above me, where it beams its dazzling adit through the air: a passageway of light that extends between the screen and the bulb, the movie and the room. If I were sitting nearer to the screen, I think, I might be able to see better. That is no doubt why my colleagues have chosen the front row. There, Dzieza, Plunkett, and Guss—arrayed like eager students at Bereyter's feet—are free to take notes by the glow of the screen. Whereas I, shrouded in secrecy and darkness at the back of the room (three rows behind the nearest person, and hidden from Bereyter), cannot see my notebook page beneath me. Until he turns the lights back on, it will be impossible to jot down my observations, criticisms, or aporia, in preparation for the Q&A. I will have to hold them all in my head until the Q&A. That is the only reason I have come to Bereyter's talk today: to destroy him, to disturb and destroy him, by posing unanswerable questions and merciless provocations throughout his Q&A. Earlier this morning, before he turned off the lights, I was able to copy down the few scant lecture notes that he had written on the whiteboard. The first item was a works-cited entry for *Vertigo*, the movie under discussion: Alfred Hitchcock, 1958, Paramount

Pictures. The second was a quotation, attributed to (what I took to be) an early lip-reading manual, *The Listening Eye*, by Dorothy Clegg: When you are deaf, Clegg writes, Bereyter wrote (and I transcribed), you live inside a well-corked glass bottle. You see the entrancing outside world, but it does not reach you. After learning to lip-read, you are still inside the bottle, but the cork has come out and the outside world slowly but surely comes in to you. The last item on the board was an aphorism by the film theorist Michel Chion: The silent film may be called the *deaf film*, Chion writes, Bereyter wrote (and I transcribed), because these films gave the moviegoer a deaf person's viewpoint on the action depicted. Listen to her, Bereyter repeats now from the lectern, his body half-turned to the canvas behind him, one hand elegantly indicating the image onscreen. He is exhorting us to *listen* to the woman seated at the bar. The clip in question keeps repeating, the same four seconds over and over. We have now had the opportunity to witness this woman mouthing her line several dozen times. While James Stewart, seated in the foreground, peers hauntedly off-camera—hoping for a glimpse of Kim Novak—the barfly in the background mutters something to her companion, smiling demurely into her drink, teasing him (or herself?) with a coquettish roll of the eyes. She is a gray-haired woman in a dark blue suit and a matching navy hat. Whatever she is saying, her dialogue remains inaudible. Her glass is empty, perhaps she is assenting to a refill. The fact is, she is not a significant character in this film. Indeed, she is not a character at all, merely an extra, with no speaking role. Though her lips move, all that can be heard on the audio track is a general murmur: the bustle of the other patrons in the bar, the clinking of drinks. Hitchcock planted her in this scene, on that barstool, and no doubt directed her to speak—to mime speech, to suggest *a scenery* of speech—but he did not position any microphone to preserve her voice. He must have told her, Say anything, anything at all, it doesn't matter, just so long as we get your mouth moving. And whatever this woman chose to say that day—there on set, in Ernie's Restaurant, in San Francisco sometime in 1957—it is now swallowed up in the ambient chatter of the scene. It has no bearing on the narrative. It is a pale utterance, a *white dialogue*. That is Bereyter's point, when he exhorts us to listen. No matter how hard we listen, nothing will be heard. Earlier this morning, in a methodological preface at the beginning of his lecture, Bereyter explained the entire process of *white dialogues* to us. First he searches for extras, he said, scouring a film's backgrounds, crowd sequences, and establishing shots for any signs of speech, any men or women whose mouths are moving. Next he isolates this footage and sends the clip to his collaborator, a lip-reading German professor at his alma mater, who analyzes the designated extras as best she can and returns her results to Bereyter in the form of a transcript. These transcripts—a handout is currently circulating the room—are apparently formatted like screenplays. In this way, Bereyter said, he excavates a parallel script, an underscript, hidden between the lines of Hitchcock's original: it is as though all this dialogue has been secretly printed there in invisible ink. Or better, he said, as if this dialogue were a message in a bottle. That is how he came to explicate the Clegg epigraph on the whiteboard: it is as though these extras, he said, have stuffed their messages into the bottles of various backgrounds, and it is only by reading their lips that we can uncork them. Since the lights were still on at that point, I was able to jot down the word *bottle* in my notebook. Only five minutes into the presentation, and already I had caught him in his first mistake. For although the movie can be said to form a kind of ontological bottle, encapsulating its characters, it is the *deaf person* (in Clegg's epigraph) who is bottled: by reading the extras' lips, it is not so much—or not only—that we rescue messages from *their* bottle; but rather, we invite them (*slowly but surely*, in Clegg's phrase) to enter the bottle that we ourselves (the *deaf moviegoers*, in Chion's phrase) are trapped inside. If the background bottle is nestled inside the *Vertigo* bottle, then both are wedged within the Wolfsegg bottle, I thought to myself, sitting silently in my desk chair. It is a *mise en abyme* of bottles, I thought, circling the word *bottle* in my notebook. Not long after this, Bereyter dimmed the lights. He began his lecture by boasting about his felicitous invention of *white dialogues*. It may come as a surprise to some of you, he said, but I discovered them quite by accident. Late one night, while rewatching *Vertigo* for my dissertation, I spotted an extra I had never noticed before. The scene (which he proceeded to screen for us) occurs twenty minutes into the film (not long after the scene at Ernie's, in fact): in it, Kim Novak visits a florist, a somehow stern-looking woman in a blue dress.

Bereyter confessed that he had watched this scene countless times beforehand, without ever registering the florist. He saw Novak mutter something to the woman, and he saw the woman nod in return. That is all. But for some reason, that night, he finally noticed what he had always failed to: the florist is speaking. Far from simply nodding at Novak, the extra is saying something to Novak. He rewound the scene repeatedly, he told us, squinting at the florist. What was she mouthing? What had she said? And would it be possible, Bereyter asked himself that night, he informed us this morning, to read her lips? After making various inquiries on campus, he eventually managed to meet the lip-reader from the German department. She agreed to review the footage, and, within a week, she had delivered her results: the florist was mouthing *All right*.

All right

At this point in his presentation, I actually picked up my pen, to try to scribble down—in the windowless Wolfsegg darkness—the phrase *All right*. But on a moment's reflection I decided that it would not be worth the trouble. These two words—this accidental scrap of dialogue, sheer happenstance dialogue, caught on camera but otherwise unintended, the improvisatory dialogue of a background florist—were meaningless. No insight could be gained into the film via this discovery. It made no contribution to Hitchcock scholarship. I was even almost embarrassed, for Bereyter. I even almost blushed, on Bereyter's behalf. *This* was what he had to show for *white dialogues*, after years of research? The silence in the room was killing. Even Dzieza, Plunkett, and

Guss—fawning there in the front row—even they must be feeling bad for Bereyter, I thought. His next example was no better. He screened for us a scene shot in a ballroom, during which he demonstrated that one dancer—a simpering man in a dark suit—could be glimpsed whispering something into the ear of his partner, an elderly woman in a ball gown of pink taffeta, outfitted with a lace tiara, perhaps the man's mother-in-law, if not his own mother, Bereyter speculated, thereby attributing filial relations and an entire backstory to these utterly inconsequential non-characters. What the simpering man turned out to be whispering, Bereyter announced, was, *If you think*.

If you think

To my great shock, this second line was not greeted with abrupt and derisive laughter, but a seism of thoughtful murmurs, which spread backward through the audience from the front row. People were genuinely impressed. I alone (evidently) had to bite my tongue. I alone (evidently) saw *white dialogues* for what they were. This was nothing more than *chitchat exegesis*, a kind of *crackpot cryptology*, I thought, watching Bereyter smile in satisfaction, as he humbly waited out the murmur. He is a charlatan, I thought. Why not close read the billboards, or the shop-window signage? I even tried to jot down the phrase *crackpot cryptology* in my journal, a little something to confront him with during the Q&A. But in the darkness all I managed to scrawl were discrete stabs of ink, stark violent hieroglyphs against the paper. And what's more, it occurred to me, setting down my pen, his methodology is not even (if I may put it this way) *sound*. Because by what criteria is his lip-reader arriving at her results? Lacking any semantic context, how is she supposed to distinguish between two homophones (*two* and *too*, for instance), or even resolve an ambiguous viseme? How was she able to tell that the florist is mouthing *all right*, rather than *all ride* or *hall write* or something else altogether? How does she distinguish one bilabial stop from another? One alveolar stop from another? One mid-front vowel from another? Could Bereyter really expect us to take this methodology seriously? No, I decided, scrawling a line back and forth in my journal: this so-called project could only be a diabolical joke, something on the order of the Sokal Hoax, cooked up by Bereyter to expose the risible state of contemporary film scholarship. I could barely believe that my colleagues—the same colleagues who have denied me tenure, referring diplomatically to my *dearth of publications* (in private they have not been so polite, I know, dismissing my single published article as deranged)—I could barely believe that Dzieza, Plunkett, and Guss were now allowing Bereyter to pull the wool so thoroughly over their eyes. He still has not moved on from the scene in Ernie's Restaurant: they are all no doubt still *listening* to the woman onscreen. My article was not deranged. Titled *Rear Window Vertigo*, it was the only chapter of my dissertation to be published, and its thesis is that *Vertigo* is in fact a *second act* or *secret sequel* to one of Hitchcock's previous films, 1954's *Rear Window*. Both movies star James Stewart, and my article's insight was that Stewart is not playing two distinct roles: rather, he is playing the same character in each film, or, more precisely, the same character in a single film, a four-hour film titled *Rear Window Vertigo*. In *Rear Window*, the first half of the film, Stewart plays a photographer and amateur detective in New York, under the name L.B. Jefferies, who spies on his neighbors with his camera's telephoto lens. In the second half of the film, *Vertigo*, he plays a professional detective in San Francisco, under the name Scottie, who is hired to shadow Kim Novak, allegedly possessed by the ghost of her great-grandmother. Jeff and Scottie, my article reasons, can only be the same person, a Scottie-Jeff hybrid, comprising two split but reciprocal identities. It is as if, at the end of *Rear Window*, Jeff undergoes some kind of psychogenic fugue: forgetting both his name and his existence, he travels in an amnesiac trance across the country, from New York to San Francisco, from *Rear Window* to *Vertigo*, where he takes up a second life as Scottie, who is then compelled to repeat key details of Jeff's repressed identity, as if possessed by him. How else to explain the uncanny continuities between these characters? For instance, their mutual fear of heights. Looked at one way, Jeff's traumatic fall from the apartment building (at the end of *Rear Window*) is what triggers Scottie's symptomatic acrophobia (at the beginning of *Vertigo*), when he finds himself dangling from a ledge for (what he does not realize is) the second time in his life.

The majority of my article is devoted to tracking down and demonstrating these kinds of correspondences, which I do ruthlessly, indisputably, despite the kneejerk dismissiveness of Dzieza, Plunkett, and Guss. There is no other explanation. James Stewart has exited *Rear Window* for *Vertigo*. He has escaped the *Rear Window* bottle for the *Vertigo* bottle. No sooner has he left the *Rear Window* frying pan than he has entered the *Vertigo* fire. Neither Scottie nor Jeff but Scottie-Jeff. That was—is—the major insight of my article. And yet it is as nothing next to Bereyter's insights, according to my colleagues, for my article is contaminated at the outset by its *enabling methodological error*. I am found guilty of ignoring the boundary line dividing these two films. Never mind the fact that that is precisely the point of my article, or that it is James Stewart himself who has ignored this boundary line. This is what counts for a methodological error, among my colleagues, rather than lip-reading. But whereas I may not have coined a flashy term for my techniques, and whereas I may not have signed a publishing contract for my dissertation with the University of N— Press—as the irrepressible departmental gossip suggests that Bereyter has—and whereas I, in my mid-thirties, still untenured, largely unpublished, am about to be cast back into the void of the anoxic job market, at least I am on the side of Hitchcock. *I* at least am close-reading *Hitchcock's* dialogue, dialogue that he approved in script, and not only that, but dialogue that he then directed the delivery of, and fastidiously positioned his microphones to record, and instructed his audio engineers to mix at a perceptible level, all so that it would play a definite and measurable role in the meaning of his movie. Unlike Bereyter, I am not engaged in some preposterous aleatoric hermeneutics; I am not attempting to somehow one-up the director himself, driven by scholarly hubris and an unsurpassed disregard for Hitchcock—not to say Hitchcock contempt, Hitchcock hostility, a transparently Oedipal and near-homicidal Hitchcock hatred—to ignore the dialogue of his design, rooting around instead inside his blind spots, hell-bent on hunting down any chance mouth movements that may have slipped into his film, between as it were the film's cracks, beneath as it were Hitchcock's watch, which—if you ask me (*no one did*)—is the methodological error par excellence. Yes, there are almost unthinkable levels of aggression wound up in *white dialogues*, aggression toward Hitchcock and aggression toward his films. Bereyter is trying to spy on Hitchcock, to expose his secrets.

White dialogues are his telephoto lens, as surely as he is Hitchcock's L.B. Jefferies. I look again at the canvas behind Bereyter. The scene at Ernie's is still flickering against it, and the woman at the bar is still mouthing her inaudible message. Whether Bereyter has already read her *white dialogue* aloud, when I wasn't paying attention, or whether he is still showboating by exhorting us to *listen to her*, I cannot discern. He appears to have moved ahead in his lecture, or perhaps he is on a tangent; at any rate he is now discussing the use of white noise in *The Birds*. Ignoring him, I continue to watch the woman at the bar. Every four seconds or so the scene jumps back to the beginning, caught in its loop. In this way she is forced to keep restarting her dialogue, forever unable to finish, like some Sisyphus of speech. It is as though this endless repetition or eternal return of the sentence is itself the sentence she is serving, the chthonic contrapasso that has been meted out to her, upon her arrival in the underworld, I think. Sitting alone in my desk chair in the darkness, at the very back of this basement seminar room, thinking of the underworld, I notice in a distracted way—and for the second time this morning—the woman's graying hair. It is then that the thought occurs to me: yes, I realize, this woman must be dead, long dead by now, her presence on the canvas spectral.

On the whiteboard beside the screen, Bereyter has not yet erased his works-cited entry. 1958. That is right: over five decades have passed since the filming of this scene, half a century, and even then she was already middle-aged. This woman on the screen before me, this woman smiling to her companion—mouthing something, rolling her eyes—this evident coquette, lush, and flirt, this actor, this extra, this filler, this specimen of *white dialogues* and therefore this woman whom Bereyter is exhorting us to listen to today, she is a dead woman. There is no getting around it. Bereyter has employed his German professor to read the lips of the dead. Whoever that actor was (her name will undoubtedly go unlisted in the credits), she could never have expected this outcome. When she agreed to occupy a barstool in the background of the new Hitchcock film, and when that esteemed Englishman directed her to speak freely, to simply improvise—no one would ever hear her, he must have told her, she enjoyed the privacy of silence—she could never have predicted that one day, half a century later, who knows how many years after her own death, some presumptuous scholar in a prep-school cardigan would be reading her lips. Whatever she said that day, she had surely assumed that it would remain a secret, whispered in confidence to her companion at the bar, her costar in quietness. After leaving the set, she probably forgot the line of dialogue herself. And when she brought her family to see *Vertigo* on opening night, and pointed out her image on the silver screen—her son leaning toward her in the darkness, asking, What are you saying there, Mother? What were you mouthing that day?—it is likely, then, that her words were as much a mystery to her as to everyone else in the theater. That she was powerless to remember. That she had stuffed this message deep into the background bottle of the scene, then promptly forgotten about it. Having consigned it to her unconscious, she must have ended up taking it—as they say—to her grave. It was to be the great secret of her life, this great silence, the private message that she had immortalized in four seconds of *Vertigo*: inviolably bottled until the end of time. Well, for half a century at least. She had not counted on Bereyter. She had failed to anticipate this eavesdropper, this grave robber, this bottle-*opener* and corkscrew artist, who decades after her death would break into *Vertigo* and extract her message himself. She had not foreseen that he would go so far as to hire a lip-reader to wrench this message from her dead lips. *Messages of the dead.* Of course— why hadn't I thought of it before? That is surely how Bereyter intends to pitch his *white dialogues* to us this morning: as transmissions from beyond, coded messages from the underworld. His sheaf of *white dialogues*, there on the lectern before him, is as ridiculous as a Ouija-board transcript. When he reads from it next, in his best campfire quaver—in his horripilating Vincent Price whisper—that, surely, will be the climax and acme of his mountebankery this morning. Listen to her, he will intone to us in a hushed voice, and *hear the messages of the dead*. Listen to her!, he will then boom out at us from the lectern, and behold this signal from beyond, which we have recovered from the white noise of death. There is to be no limit to his presumptuousness: not only a savant, but a visionary; not only a pedant, but a necromancer. That is the raison d'être of his *white dialogues*, necromancy pure and simple. This woman at the bar cannot be the only corpse in *Vertigo*, after all. After half a century, most of its cast must be dead. James Stewart, I know, died of a pulmonary embolism in 1997. The florist is obviously dead, and the simpering dancer too (to say nothing of his elderly mother-in-law, or mother, who probably perished in the parking lot mere seconds after stepping off set). Kim Novak alone (evidently) is not yet dead. But as for everyone else, almost every other extra, they are all cadavers now, if not completely decomposed. *Skeletons in their coffins*, I think, in an utterly morbid tone of mind-voice, and this thought seems to penetrate the image onscreen like an X-ray, transforming the very extras at the bar into a band of skeletons, such that the restaurant strikes me for a moment as the most grotesque apotheosis of death, a horde of corpses.

A horde of corpses

James Stewart with his haunted expression is dead, and the balding man at the bar behind him (his blonde hair brushed back from his calvity) dead, and the romantic trio in the background (the woman in the dovegray pea coat, her date in his charcoal suit, the tall gentleman chaperoning the two of them) every one of them dead, struck down by the last half century. Chatting convivially on set, they too are likely victims of Bereyter's grave robbery. For that is what his *white dialogues* project amounts to, in the final analysis: already hermeneutically useless, already methodologically unsound, it is also, after all that, sheer vandalism; it is also, on top of everything else, the most depraved and tasteless tomb raiding. I watch the dead woman at the bar. I imagine her son watching this movie, now that she is dead. He must replay this scene on repeat as well, from time to time. If nothing else about his mother is certain, these four seconds present an irrefutable truth: one day in 1957, on set in Ernie's Restaurant in San Francisco, *she was there*. Her klieg-lit body reflected luminous rays, which were captured in the canisters of Hitchcock's camera, and with the breath of her lungs she uttered various words, which no microphones recorded. That is the paradox of film: on the one hand, she is dead; but on the other hand she is still—inside these four seconds—alive. Sitting at the bar, flickering on this screen, she is not *yet* dead. It is 1957, her death lies beyond the horizon of the film, she has forever yet to die. *She is dead, and she is going to die,* her son must mutter softly to himself, while rewinding this scene on the DVD, I think. This movie, for him, must be no different from any other family album or home video. It is a photographic document of his living mother: the treasury of her rays, a last surviving locket of her light. The one thing it did not preserve—the one thing this footage cannot tell him—is what she said that day. And so thank God for Bereyter: thank God Bereyter has finally arrived at *Vertigo*, crowbar in hand, to pry the lid off this poor woman's sepulcher. Thank God he has crawled deep inside—accompanied by his ghoulish lip-reading Igor—to plunder her message once and for all. And he won't stop there: next he will publish his results with the University of N—, ensuring that this bereaved man can one day flip through the pages of Bereyter's book and find his dead mother's image printed in a screen capture, with an italicized caption floating beneath her face. At long last, at this late date, he will be able to see—laid bare in all their banality, their bathos—the words his dead mother spoke that day: *Yes, I'll have another*; *No thank you*; *All right.* If I could see my notebook in this darkness, I think, gripping my pen pointlessly, if only I could see, I would sketch a quick caricature of Bereyter now. Yes, that would give me ultimate pleasure. To portray Bereyter as he truly is: not in his prep-school cardigan, but in his khaki bush jacket and pith helmet; not with his sheaf of lecture notes, but wielding his pickaxe, his loot sack, as he tears open this poor woman's sarcophagus. For *Vertigo* is her pyramid, as surely as Bereyter is her Howard Carter. Of course all films—but especially old films—are pyramids, I realize. Of course all films—but especially old films—serve a preservative function: they exist first and foremost to freeze-dry their actors' bodies, safeguarding them from destruction. I know this as well as anyone. Actors' heads are shrunken in the formaldehyde jars of close-ups. They are embalmed within the film, mummified by the film. That is why it is possible to view all films—but especially old films—as mummy films. Photography began, after all, as a mummifying technology, a 19th-century advance in mankind's age-old mummy complex. With each passing era, I know, mankind has perfected the perverse art of preserving corpses. First the mummy, then the death mask, then the photograph. After the photograph, there remained only one logical step: the moving image. From Egypt down to the Egyptian Theater, there has been a direct and unbroken lineage. Every movie is a pyramid, stuffed tight with mummies. Every movie is a mobile gallery of death masks. I have always felt this way. Whereas most viewers see actors' faces, all I see are death masks. Whereas my colleagues are liable to say, *That actor did a fine job,* I always have to stop myself from saying, *That death mask did a fine job. Frankly, my dear,* I hear one death mask say to the other death mask, *I don't give a damn,* and I watch in horror as tears stream down the second death mask's face. With *Vertigo* it is no different. I see the James Stewart death mask kiss the Kim Novak death mask. I see the pulmonary-embolism death mask kiss the not-yet death mask. Even though Kim Novak is still alive, her face in this movie is no less grotesque a death mask: it is a twenty-five-year-old's death mask, a simulacral death mask, waiting patiently for its living counterpart to die. Meanwhile, in the backgrounds of these scenes, there are whole crowds of death masks, every shot a charnel house of death masks, the unmummified or half-mummified faces of extras. It is as in any pyramid: here too there are hierarchies of preservation. At the pharaonic apex, there are Stewart and Novak, painstakingly embalmed. Not only their images, but their voices as well, have been extended into eternity. Below them are the extras, their servants and courtiers, who have been permitted to disintegrate. Sometimes the camera does not bother to preserve these extras' faces, only a passing shoulder, a half-turned back. Sometimes their voices have been excluded from the audio track. Everywhere the movie echoes like a mausoleum with the sounds of Stewart's voice, which drowns out all the extras' voices, such that we cannot hear what these people are saying. For over half a century, their speech has remained invisible: un-listened-to, and perhaps unlistenable, buried beneath the phenomenal threshold of the film. Their names are not even listed in the film's credits. In these so-called credits—in fact they are necrologies—in these crawling columns of the dead, the extras do not merit registry. They are the plebeian dead, anonymous corpses. Faceless, mute, they have been lost to nameless oblivion. Now, half a century later, Bereyter has arrived to disturb their rest.

The pulmonary-embolism death mask kisses the not-yet death mask

At the lectern, Bereyter is silent. He frowns down at his notes, apparently pausing for emphasis. Then he glances up and clears his throat: If you listen to this woman, he finally announces, you will hear only the surrounding drone of Ernie's Restaurant. But this drone, he goes on, is diegetic: it is as deafening for the characters as it is for us. This man at the bar, he says, this woman's companion, he is leaning forward to hear her, in fact must be struggling to hear her, and perhaps he is even reading her lips himself. Bereyter smiles coyly here. In forcing us to squint at her lips, he continues, the film gives us a deaf person's viewpoint on the action depicted. As in a silent movie, this woman portrays a character whose lips must be read. Which is all the more remarkable, Bereyter concludes, when we finally discover what she is mouthing. For she is the first self-conscious author of a metafictional or metatextual *white dialogue*, a self-referential *white dialogue*. He holds up his left hand now, to indicate a direct quotation, and then—looking down at the lectern—begins to read: *Read my lips*, this woman says, Bereyter says. *It's Jeff.*

Read my lips: it's Jeff

There is another excited murmur in the audience. Bereyter projects his voice over the uproar: She has embraced her silence, he booms out at us from the lectern, qua *white dialogue*. Knowing that Hitchcock has placed her in a zone of white noise, he says, she commands her companion to read her lips. At this point Bereyter presses on with his lecture, expatiating on the implications of her utterance. But I am no longer listening. I am still watching the clip on the screen. Bereyter leaves it looping on the canvas behind him, and I cannot tear my eyes from the dead woman. Read my lips, she is saying, it's Jeff. And when I study her lips, yes, it is obvious, that is what she has been mouthing all along. *Read my lips*, it is as plain as day. *Read my lips*, I read, pressing my body against the back of my chair. *It's Jeff*, I read, pushing against the edge of my desktop with both hands. Bereyter babbles on at the lectern, oblivious. He has no clue what he has uncovered. The dead woman looms huge behind him—spectral, repetitive, looping her impossible message over and over—and Bereyter gestures left and right, lecturing to his audience. He is incapable of appreciating the significance of his own discovery. For while glancing sidelong at James Stewart—how had I not noticed?—this woman is mouthing, *It's Jeff*. She is referring to Stewart, not as Scottie, but as Jeff: his repressed name, his *Rear Window* name. It is as if some background actor, some extra from *Rear Window*, has *followed James Stewart into the film*. As if this woman in her blue suit has herself traveled all the way from New York to San Francisco, from *Rear Window* to *Vertigo*, shadowing Scottie-Jeff to Ernie's. Spotting him there, she identifies him. There is no other explanation. *Read my lips: it's Jeff.* This message she is mouthing, directly toward the screen, is meant not for her companion, but for the audience. She is telling the audience—*she is telling me*—that Scottie is an impostor, that he is actually Jeff, a hybrid or chimerical Scottie-Jeff, she is confirming my theory in the most incontrovertible terms. It is undeniable now: there *is* no border between these films. James Stewart and this extra have both succeeded in escaping. They have left the *Rear Window* bottle for the *Vertigo* bottle. They have abandoned the *Rear Window* pyramid for the *Vertigo* pyramid. And what is to stop her, I wonder—regarding her image warily on the screen—what is to stop her from leaving the *Vertigo* bottle for the Wolfsegg bottle? Now that Bereyter has uncorked her? What is to keep her from escaping through the adit of the projector shaft, and from crawling (*slowly but surely*, in Clegg's phrase) out of the movie and into the room? I close my eyes, unable to watch, and by the time I reopen them I have stopped breathing. But she is still sitting there of course, trapped on the flatness of the screen. The dead woman looks into my eyes, telling me again and again to read her lips, repeating over and over that it's Jeff. I am entirely too agitated to stay. Without taking my eyes from hers, I rise from my chair in a single stealthy motion. Except I must make a noise, for the man a few rows ahead of me turns around. Seeing me standing there, he holds up an index finger, imploring me to wait a moment, then twists in his seat to grab a sheet of paper from his desk. He reaches across the aisle to give it to me. Taking it, I nod my head in thanks and sit back down. I don't have time for this, I tell myself, even as I am placing the paper on my desktop; I have to get out of here, I think, even as I am smoothing it flat with my hand. It is a column of three photographs, screen captures from *Vertigo*, with italicized captions printed beneath them. The lip-reader's transcript. I scan the extras' faces, looking for any refugees from *Rear Window*. By the flickering of the projector, I squint down at the captions, straining to read their *white dialogues*.

Sommelier: But if you don't stop—of course

Barman: I'll be right there, be right there

Diner 1: We see you

I recognize the scene immediately. It occurs midway through the film, during Scottie-Jeff's return to Ernie's Restaurant. Again he takes his place on the barstool, peering hauntedly off-camera. Again the corpses around him mutter among themselves. I skim their captions quickly, three times in succession, looking for any clues. But none of them call out, *It's Jeff!* Instead, the sommelier confers with the host. The barman attends to his bespectacled patron. *But if you do not stop*, says the one; *I'll be right there*, says the other. As for Diner 1—who I can only presume is the wolfish man in the black bowtie—he is holding forth at his table, grinning mischievously at the woman seated opposite him. *We see you*, he tells her. *We see you*, he says. I shake my head at the transcript. Bereyter could not have written less meaningful *white dialogues* himself. And yet, I think, rereading the captions for the fourth time, there is something not quite right here. Something in each screen capture—something ineffable— is off: each frame before me bears some uncanny incongruity. Perhaps it is only because my eye has been trained by Hitchcock, conditioned to seek out the one stray detail that unsettles the image—the crop duster dusting a cropless field; the windmill that spins against the breeze—but it strikes me that these cannot possibly be the words that the extras are mouthing. The sommelier, flaunting a wine bottle in his hands, admonishes the host with this enigmatic ultimatum: *If you do not stop*, he says... But stop what? Meanwhile the barman assures his customer—even as he is walking away from him—*I'll be right there, be right there.* Then there is Diner 1: he tells the woman, *We see you*, when no one at the table is even looking at her. He himself is glancing—grinning—at a point over her shoulder. There must be some mistake. The lip-reader must have misread their lips. The barman could very well be mouthing, *Pee right there.* I mouth these syllables silently to myself, testing out the alternatives. *Fright there*, I mouth to myself, and then, *Bright air. Bright star*, I mouth to myself, and then, *Be right air. Be right err, Be rye tare*, I mouth to myself, as a chill runs through me. *Be reyt er*, I mouth to myself, gripping my pen, *Bereyter. Right there*, I mouth to myself, *Bereyter. Right there, Bereyter*, I mouth to myself. Pen in hand, I scrawl a line through the italicized caption, forcefully crossing out the second *be right there*. Beside it I write—as best I can in the darkness, my hand trembling—*Bereyter.*

I'll be right there, ~~be right there~~ Bereyter

Yes. Yes. It is insane, but it is obvious. In fact it is even more obvious than it is insane. *That* is what the barman is mouthing. He is speaking not to his customer, but to Bereyter. He is on his way—not to his customer—*but to Bereyter*. And the other extras as well. For instance the sommelier with his wine bottle, mouthing *But if you don't stop*. Who else could he be addressing, besides Bereyter? What else could this even mean, besides, *If you don't stop disturbing our rest? If you don't stop uncorking our deaths, the silent bottle that our death is, as vulnerable as this bottle that I hold in my hands?* If you don't stop, of course, I'll be right there, Bereyter. *We see you.* I look at the transcript in horror: Diner 1's beady eyes stare far past his companion's shoulder, peering out of the paper to pierce my own. It is unmistakable: he is looking straight through the camera and has been looking through that camera for fifty years, patiently, unblinkingly, waiting for the day when someone would finally meet his gaze. When someone would trespass this border and demolish this fourth wall. *We see you*, he says, *We see you*, speaking not just for his tablemates, but—it dawns on me—every single extra in *Vertigo*, such that now, all at once, the grin on his face takes on the most sinister dimensions. My God, I think, staring down dumbfounded at the transcript on my desk… *They are coming.* At just this moment, the lights flash on. I blink furiously, blinded by the sudden fluorescence, and I see that Bereyter—having stepped from behind the lectern—is now pushing up the navy sleeves of his cardigan. He is initiating the Q&A. Behind him, the canvas is blank; above me, the projector is no longer whirring. A hand shoots up in the front row, either Dzieza's, Plunkett's, or Guss's, it does not matter. I cannot bear to listen. Bereyter has invited the wrath of the dead upon all of us. He has broken into the mummy's pyramid, broken the seal on the mummy's tomb. He has called down the mummy's curse on all our heads, and no one else understands this. Oh, I have questions for Bereyter all right. I have been storing them up all morning. I begin to write them in my notebook, just beneath the word *bottle*. My hand scribbles compulsively, building up its case against Bereyter. At the critical moment, I will have to rise from this seat at the back of the room, where I have gone unnoticed in the shadows, and then I alone (evidently) will have to confront Bereyter with the monstrousness of what he's done. *Yes, yes,* he will call, *you there, in the back,* and I will pose the questions that my colleagues are unable to, the questions that my hand—even now—is scrawling in my notebook beneath me. Have you no decency, Bereyter?, I will ask. What did you think would happen, Bereyter?, I will ask. How did you expect the dead to react, when you and your lip-reader went uncorking them? When you opened the lid, not on Pandora's Box, Bereyter, but on Pandora's Bottle? Not on Pandora's *Pithos*, Bereyter, but on Pandora's Pyramid? Bereyter, Bereyter, what have you done? I let the pen fall from my hand. It goes rolling over the side of the desktop, clattering to the floor. Rising to my feet, I grip the chair to steady myself, and concentrate all the energy in my being. Yes, I hear Bereyter call from the front of the room, you there. In the back.

Acknowledgments

My thanks to the following institutions for their generosity and hospitality: Bard College, especially Leon Botstein, Mary Caponegro, Wout Cornelissen, Benjamin Hale, Robert Kelly, Grayson Morley, Micaela Morrissette, Bradford Morrow, Francine Prose, Raissa St. Pierre, and Irene Zedlacher; the Copernicus Society of America; the Iowa Writers' Workshop, especially Connie Brothers, Kelly Smith, Deb West, and Jan Zenisek; the MacDowell Colony; the Truman Capote Literary Trust, especially Louise Schwartz; the University of Iowa English Department, especially Brooks Landon and Robyn Schiff; and the Corporation of Yaddo, especially Elaina Richardson and Candace Wait.

Thank you to Roni Lubliner and Peer Ebbighausen at NBCUniversal, and to Leland Faust at the Alfred J. Hitchcock Trust, for permission and assistance in reproducing images from Hitchcock's films.

Thanks as well to the following readers for their insight and support: Jin Auh, Andrés Carlstein, Bryan Castille, Daniel Castro, Adam Eaglin, E.J. Fischer, Angela Flournoy, Jessica Friedman, Meg Gauley, Susan Hazen-Hammond, Arna Hemenway, Brigid Hughes, Evan Michael James, T. Geronimo Johnson, Cheston Knapp, Aaron Kunin, Travis Kurowski, David Leavitt, Carmen Maria Machado, Kannan Mahadevan, Halimah Marcus, Erica Martz, Ayana Mathis, Mark Mayer, Eric Obenauf, Amy Parker, Michael Ray, Marilynne Robinson, Rebecca Rukeyser, Jennifer Sahn, Pat Sims, Harry Stecopoulos, Wells Tower, Tony Tulathimutte, Madhuri Vijay, Adrian Van Young, and Eliza Jane Wood. Special thanks to Sam Chang and Ben Mauk.

'White Dialogues' quotes or paraphrases several works of film theory. The 'Rear Window Vertigo' reading is Jalal Toufic's, from his essay 'Rear Window Vertigo,' included in *Two or Three Things I'm Dying To Tell You*. The phrase (and the concept of) 'the mummy complex' is André Bazin's, from his essay 'The Ontology of the Photographic Image,' included in *What Is Cinema? Vol. 1*. The formulation 'she is dead, and she is going to die' (as well as some of the surrounding language in that passage) is Roland Barthes's, from *Camera Lucida*. The Michel Chion quotation is a combination of two separate passages, both from *The Voice in Cinema*.

The phrase (and the concept of) 'radical closure' is Jalal Toufic's.

Two Dollar Radio
Books too loud to Ignore

ALSO AVAILABLE Here are some other titles you might want to dig into.

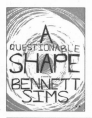

A QUESTIONABLE SHAPE NOVEL BY **BENNETT SIMS**

→ **Best Books 2013:** *Slate, Salon,* NPR's 'On Point'

← "Certainly the first Proustian zombie novel, but hopefully not the last horror novel of ideas." —*Slate*

SIMS TURNS TYPICAL ZOMBIE fare on its head to deliver a wise and philosophical rumination on the nature of memory and loss, as a young man searches for his disappeared father in Baton Rouge.

HOW TO GET INTO THE TWIN PALMS
NOVEL BY **KAROLINA WACLAWIAK**

← "Reinvents the immigration story." —*New York Times Book Review*

ANYA IS A YOUNG WOMAN living in a Russian neighborhood in LA, torn between her parents' Polish heritage and trying to assimilate in the U.S. She decides instead to try and assimilate in her Russian community, embodied by the nightclub, the Twin Palms.

THE ONLY ONES NOVEL BY **CAROLA DIBBELL**

→ **Best Books 2015:** *Washington Post*; *O, The Oprah Magazine*; NPR

← "Breathtaking." —NPR

INEZ WANDERS A POST-PANDEMIC world immune to disease. Her life is altered when a grief-stricken mother that hired her to provide genetic material backs out, leaving Inez with the product: a baby girl.

SEEING PEOPLE OFF NOVEL BY **JANA BEŇOVÁ**

→ **Winner of the European Union Prize for Literature**

← "A fascinating novel. Fans of inward-looking postmodernists like Clarice Lispector will find much to admire." —NPR

A KALEIDOSCOPIC, POETIC, AND DARKLY FUNNY portrait of a young couple navigating post-socialist Slovakia.

Thank you for supporting independent culture!
Feel good about yourself.

Books to read!

Now available at **TWODOLLARRADIO.com** or your favorite bookseller.

THE VINE THAT ATE THE SOUTH
NOVEL BY **J.D. WILKES**

← "Undeniably one of the smartest, most original Southern Gothic novels to come along in years." —NPR

WITH THE ENERGY AND UNIQUE VISION that established him as a celebrated musician, Wilkes here is an accomplished storyteller on a Homeric voyage that strikes at the heart of American mythology.

THE DROP EDGE OF YONDER
NOVEL BY **RUDOLPH WURLITZER**

← "One of the most interesting voices in American fiction." —*Rolling Stone*

WURLITZER'S FIRST NOVEL in nearly 25 years is an epic adventure that explores the truth and temptations of the American myth, revealing one of America's most transcendant writers at the top of his form.

SQUARE WAVE NOVEL BY **MARK DE SILVA**

← "Compelling and horrifying." —*Chicago Tribune*

A GRAND NOVEL OF ideas and compelling crime mystery, about security states past and present, weather modification science, micro-tonal music, and imperial influences.

BABY GEISHA STORIES BY **TRINIE DALTON**

← "[The stories] feel like brilliant sexual fairy tales on drugs. Dalton writes of self-discovery and sex with a knowing humility and humor." —*Interview Magazine*

Did high school English ruin you? Do you like movies that make you cry? Are you looking for a strong female voice? Zombies? We've got you covered with the Two Dollar Radio Flowchart. By answering a series of questions, find your new favorite book today! ⇢ TWODOLLARRADIO.COM/PAGES/FLOWCHART

Two Dollar Radio
Books too loud to Ignore

ALSO AVAILABLE Here are some other titles you might want to dig into.

THE REACTIVE NOVEL BY **MASANDE NTSHANGA**

← "Often teems with a beauty that seems to carry on in front of its glue-huffing wasters despite themselves." —*Slate*

A CLEAR-EYED, COMPASSIONATE ACCOUNT of a young HIV+ man grappling with the sudden death of his brother in South Africa.

THE GLOAMING NOVEL BY **MELANIE FINN**

→ *New York Times* **Notable Book of 2016**

← "Deeply satisfying." —*New York Times Book Review*

AFTER AN ACCIDENT LEAVES her estranged in a Swiss town, Pilgrim Jones absconds to east Africa, settling in a Tanzanian outpost where she can't shake the unsettling feeling that she's being followed.

MIRA CORPORA NOVEL BY **JEFF JACKSON**

→ *Los Angeles Times* **Book Prize Finalist**

← "A piercing howl of a book." —*Slate*

A COMING OF AGE story for people who hate coming of age stories, featuring a colony of outcast children, teenage oracles, amusement parks haunted by gibbons, and mysterious cassette tapes.

SIRENS MEMOIR BY **JOSHUA MOHR**

← "Raw-edged and whippet-thin... A featherweight boxer that packs a punch." —*Los Angeles Times*

WITH VULNERABILITY, GRIT, AND HARD-WON HUMOR, acclaimed novelist Joshua Mohr returns with his first book-length work of non-fiction, a raw and big-hearted chronicle of substance abuse, relapse, and family compassion.

SOME RECOMMENDED LOCATIONS FOR READING TWO DOLLAR RADIO BOOKS:

On a beach, in the dark, using a lighter's flame; While getting a tattoo of an ex-lover's name removed; While painting the toe nails of someone you love; Or, pretty much anywhere because books are portable and the perfect technology!